Unmatched and unbroken

He was a giant of a horse, glistening black—too big to be pure Arabian. The head was that of the wildest of all wild creatures—a stallion born wild—and it was beautiful, savage, splendid. A stallion with a wonderful physical perfection that matched his savage, ruthless spirit.

Once again the Black screamed and rose on his hind legs. Alec could hardly believe his eyes and ears—a stallion, a wild stallion—unbroken, such as he had read and dreamed about!

"The Black Stallion is about the most famous
fictional horse of the century."
—*New York Times*

The Black Stallion
The Black Stallion and Flame
The Black Stallion and Satan
The Black Stallion and the Girl
The Black Stallion Legend
The Black Stallion Mystery
The Black Stallion Returns
The Black Stallion's Blood Bay Colt
The Black Stallion's Courage
Son of the Black Stallion
The Young Black Stallion

The Black Stallion

WALTER FARLEY

BULLSEYE BOOKS · RANDOM HOUSE · NEW YORK

To Mother, Dad, and Bill

Contents

Homeward Bound

1

The tramp steamer *Drake* plowed away from the coast of India and pushed its blunt prow into the Arabian Sea, homeward bound. Slowly it made its way west toward the Gulf of Aden. Its hold was loaded with coffee, rice, tea, oil seeds and jute. Black smoke poured from its one stack, darkening the hot cloudless sky.

Alexander Ramsay, known to his friends back home in New York City as Alec, leaned over the rail and watched the water slide away from the sides of the boat. His red hair blazed redder than ever in the hot sun; his tanned elbows rested heavily on the rail as he turned his freckled face back toward the fast-disappearing shore.

It had been fun—those two months in India. He would miss Uncle Ralph, miss the days they had spent together in the jungle, even the screams of the panthers and the many eerie sounds of the jungle night. Never again would he think of a missionary's work as easy work. No, sir, you had to be big and strong, able to ride horseback for long hours through the tangled jungle paths. Alec glanced down proudly at the hard muscles in his arms. Uncle Ralph had taught him how to ride—the one thing in the world he had always wanted to do.

But it was all over now. Rides back home would be few.

His fist opened. Lovingly he surveyed the pearl pocketknife he held there. The inscription on it was in gold: *To Alec on his birthday, Bombay, India.* He remembered, too, his uncle's words: "A knife, Alec, comes in handy sometimes."

Suddenly a large hand descended on his shoulder. "Well, m'boy, you're on your way home," a gruff voice said, with a decidedly English accent.

Alec looked up into the captain's wrinkled, windtanned face. "Hello, Captain Watson," he answered. "It's rather a long way home, though, sir. To England with you and then to New York on the *Majestic.*"

"About four weeks' sailing, all in all, lad, but you look like a pretty good sailor."

"I am, sir. I wasn't sick once all the way over and we had a rough crossing, too," Alec said proudly.

"When'd you come over, lad?"

"In June, sir, with some friends of my father's. They left me with my uncle in Bombay. You know my Uncle Ralph, don't you? He came aboard with me and spoke to you."

"Yes, I know your Uncle Ralph. A fine man, too. . . . And now you're going home alone?"

"Yes, sir! School opens next month and I have to be there."

The captain smiled and took Alec by the arm. "Come along," he said. "I'll show you how we steer this ship and what makes it go."

The captain and crew were kind to Alec, but the days passed monotonously for the homeward-bound boy as the *Drake* steamed its way through the Gulf of Aden and into the Red Sea. The tropic sun beat down mercilessly on the heads of the few passengers aboard.

The *Drake* kept near the coast of Arabia—endless miles of barren desert shore. But Alec's thoughts were not on the scorching sand. Arabia—where the greatest horses in the world were bred! Did other fellows dream of horses the way he did? To him, a horse was the greatest animal in the world.

Then one day the *Drake* headed for a small Arabian port. As they approached the small landing, Alec saw a crowd of Arabs milling about in great excitement. Obviously it was not often that a boat stopped there.

But, as the gangplank went down with a bang, Alec could see that it wasn't the ship itself that was attracting all the attention. The Arabs were crowding toward the center of the landing. Alec heard a whistle—shrill, loud, clear, unlike anything he had ever heard before. He saw a mighty black horse rear on its hind legs, its forelegs striking out into the air. A white scarf was tied across its eyes. The crowd broke and ran.

White lather ran from the horse's body; his mouth was open, his teeth bared. He was a giant of a horse, glistening black—too big to be pure Arabian. His mane was like a crest, mounting, then falling low. His neck was long and slender, and arched to the small, savagely beautiful head. The head was that of the wildest of all wild creatures—a stallion born wild—and it was beautiful, savage, splendid. A stallion with a wonderful physical perfection that matched his savage, ruthless spirit.

Once again the Black screamed and rose on his hind legs. Alec could hardly believe his eyes and ears—a stallion, a wild stallion—unbroken, such as he had read and dreamed about!

Two ropes led from the halter on the horse's head, and four men were attempting to pull the stallion toward the gangplank. They were going to put him on the ship! Alec saw a dark-skinned man, wearing European dress and a high, white turban, giving directions. In his hand he held a whip. He gave his orders tersely in Arabic. Suddenly he walked to the rear of the horse and let the hard whip fall on the Black's hindquarters. The stallion bolted so fast that he struck one of the Arabs holding the rope; down the man went and lay still. The Black snorted and plunged; if ever Alec saw hate expressed by a horse, he saw it then. They had him halfway up the plank. Alec wondered where they would put him if they ever did succeed in getting him on the boat.

Then he was on! Alec saw Captain Watson waving his arms frantically, motioning and shouting for the men to pull the stallion toward the stern. The boy followed at a safe distance. Now he saw the makeshift stall into which they were attempting to get the Black—it had once been a good-sized cabin. The *Drake* had little accommodation for transporting animals; its hold was already heavily laden with cargo.

Finally they had the horse in front of the stall. One of the men clambered to the top of the cabin, reached down and pulled the scarf away from the stallion's eyes. At the same time, the dark-skinned man again hit the horse on the hindquarters and he bolted inside. Alec thought the stall would never be strong enough to hold him. The stallion tore into the wood and sent it flying; thunder rolled from under his hoofs; his powerful legs crashed into the sides of the cabin; his wild, shrill, high-pitched whistle filled the air. Alec felt a deep pity steal over him, for here was a wild stallion used to the open range imprisoned in a stall in which he was hardly able to turn.

Captain Watson was conversing angrily with the dark-skinned man; the captain had probably never expected to ship a cargo such as this! Then the man pulled a thick wallet from inside his coat; he counted the bills off and handed them to the captain. Captain Watson looked at the bills and then at the stall; he took the money, shrugged his shoulders and walked away. The dark-skinned man gathered the Arabs who had helped bring the stallion aboard, gave them bills from his wallet, and they departed down the gangplank.

Soon the *Drake* was again under way. Alec gazed back at the port, watching the group gathered around the inert form of the Arab who had gone down under the Black's mighty hoofs; then he turned to the stall. The dark-skinned man had gone to his cabin, and only the excited passengers were standing around outside the stall. The black horse was still fighting madly inside.

The days that followed were hectic ones for Alec, passengers and crew. He had never dreamed a horse could have such spirit, be so untamable. The ship resounded far into the night from the blows struck by those powerful legs. The outside of the stall was now covered with reinforcements. The dark-skinned man became more mysterious than ever—always alone, and never talking to anyone but the captain.

The *Drake* steamed through the Suez into the Mediterranean.

That night Alec stole out upon deck, leaving the rest of the passengers playing cards. He listened carefully. The Black was quiet tonight. Quickly he walked in the direction of the stall. At first he couldn't see or hear anything. Then as his eyes became accustomed to the darkness, he made out the pink-colored nostrils of the Black, who was sticking his head out of the window.

Alec walked slowly toward him; he put one hand in his pocket to see if the lumps of sugar he had taken from the dinner table were still there. The wind was blowing against him, carrying his scent away. He was quite close now. The Black was looking out on the open sea; his ears pricked forward, his thin-skinned nostrils quivering, his black mane flowing like windswept flame. Alec could not turn his eyes away; he could not believe such a perfect animal existed.

The stallion turned and looked directly at him—his black eyes blazed. Once again that piercing whistle filled the night air, and he disappeared into the stall. Alec took the sugar out of his pocket and left it on the window sill. He went to his cabin. Later, when he returned, it was gone. Every night thereafter Alec would steal up to the stall, leave the sugar and depart; sometimes he would see the Black and other times he would only hear the ring of hoofs against the floor.

The Storm

2

The *Drake* stopped at Alexandria, Bengasi, Tripoli, Tunis and Algiers, passed the Rock of Gibraltar and turned north up the coast of Portugal. Now they were off Cape Finisterre on the coast of Spain, and in a few days, Captain Watson told Alec, they would be in England.

Alec wondered why the Black was being shipped to England—perhaps for stud, perhaps to race. The slanting shoulders, the deep broad chest, the powerful legs, the knees not too high nor too low—these, his uncle had taught him, were marks of speed and endurance.

That night Alec made his customary trip to the stall, his pockets filled with lumps of sugar. The night was hot and still; heavy clouds blacked out the stars; in the distance long streaks of lightning raced through the sky. The Black had his head out the window. Again he was looking out to sea, his nostrils quivering more than ever. He turned, whistled as he saw the boy, then again faced the water.

Alec felt elated—it was the first time that the stallion hadn't drawn back into the stall at sight of him. He moved closer. He put the sugar in the palm of his hand and hesitantly held it out to the stallion. The Black turned and once again whistled—softer this time. Alec stood his ground. Neither he nor anyone else had been this close to the stallion since he came on board. But he did not care to take the chance of extending his arm any nearer the bared teeth, the curled nostrils. Instead he placed the sugar on the sill. The Black looked at it, then back at the boy. Slowly he moved over and began to eat the sugar. Alec watched him for a moment, satisfied; then as the rain began to fall, he went back to his cabin.

He was awakened with amazing suddenness in the middle of the night. The *Drake* lurched crazily and he was thrown onto the floor. Outside there were loud rolls of thunder, and streaks of lightning made his cabin as light as day.

His first storm at sea! He pushed the light switch—it was dead. Then a flash of lightning again illuminated the cabin. The top of his bureau had been swept clear and the floor was covered with broken glass. Hurriedly he pulled on his pants and shirt and started for the door; then he stopped. Back he went to the bed, fell on his knees and reached under. He withdrew a life jacket and strapped it around him. He hoped that he wouldn't need it.

He opened the door and made his way, staggering, to the deck. The fury of the storm drove him back into the passageway; he hung on to the stair rail and peered into the black void. He heard the shouts of Captain Watson and the crew faintly above the roar of the winds. Huge waves swept from one end of the *Drake* to the other. Hysterical passengers crowded into the corridor. Alec was genuinely scared now; never had he seen a storm like this!

For what seemed hours, the *Drake* plowed through wave after wave, trembling, careening on its side, yet somehow managing to stay afloat. The long streaks of lightning never diminished; zigzagging through the sky, their sharp cracks resounded on the water.

From the passageway, Alec saw one of the crew make his way along the deck in his direction, desperately fighting to hold on to the rail. The *Drake* rolled sideways and a huge wave swept over the boat. When it had passed, the sailor was gone. The boy closed his eyes and prayed.

The storm began to subside a little and Alec felt new hope. Then suddenly a bolt of fire seemed to fall from the heavens above them. A sharp crack and the boat shook. Alec was thrown flat on his face, stunned. Slowly he regained consciousness. He was lying on his stomach; his face felt hot and sticky. He raised his hand, and withdrew it covered with blood. Then he became conscious of feet stepping on him. The passengers, yelling and screaming, were climbing, crawling over him! The *Drake* was still— its engines dead.

Struggling, Alec pushed himself to his feet. Slowly he made his way along the deck. His startled eyes took in the scene about him. The *Drake*, struck by lightning, seemed almost cut in half! They were sinking! Strange, with what seemed the end so near, he should feel so calm. They were manning the lifeboats, and Captain Watson was there shouting directions. One boat was being lowered into the water. A large wave caught it broadside and turned it over—its occupants disappeared in the sea.

The second lifeboat was being filled and Alec waited his turn. But when it came, the boat had reached its quota.

"Wait for the next one, Alec," Captain Watson said sternly. He put his arm on the boy's shoulder, softening the harshness of his words.

As they watched the second lifeboat being lowered, the dark-skinned man appeared and rushed up to the captain, waving his arms and babbling hysterically.

"It's under the bed, under the bed!" Captain Watson shouted at him.

Then Alec saw the man had no life jacket. Terror in his eyes, he turned away from the captain toward Alec. Frantically he rushed at the boy and tried to tear the life jacket from his back. Alec struggled, but he was no match for the half-crazed man. Then Captain Watson had his hands on the man and threw him against the rail.

Alec saw the man's eyes turn to the lifeboat that was being lowered. Before the captain could stop him, he was climbing over the rail. He was going to jump into the boat! Suddenly the *Drake* lurched. The man lost his balance and, screaming, fell into the water. He never rose to the surface.

The dark-skinned man had drowned. Immediately Alec thought of the Black. What was happening to him? Was he still in his stall? Alec fought his way out of line and toward the stern of the boat. If the stallion was alive, he was going to set him free and give him his chance to fight for life.

The stall was still standing. Alec heard a shrill whistle rise above the storm. He rushed to the door, lifted the heavy bar and swung it open. For a second the mighty hoofs stopped pounding and there was silence. Alec backed slowly away.

Then he saw the Black, his head held high, his nostrils blown out with excitement. Suddenly he snorted and plunged straight for the rail and Alec. Alec was paralyzed, he couldn't move. One hand was on the rail, which was broken at this point, leaving nothing between him and the open water. The Black swerved as he came near him, and the boy realized that the stallion was making for the hole. The horse's shoulder grazed him as he swerved, and Alec went flying into space. He felt the water close over his head.

When he came up, his first thought was of the ship; then he heard an explosion, and he saw the *Drake* settling deep into the water. Frantically he looked around for a lifeboat, but there was none in sight. Then he saw the Black swimming not more than ten yards away. Something swished by him—a rope, and it was attached to the Black's halter! The same rope that they had used to bring the stallion aboard the boat, and which they had never been able to get close enough to the horse to untie. Without stopping to think, Alec grabbed hold of it. Then he was pulled through the water, into the oncoming seas.

The waves were still large, but with the aid of his life jacket, Alec was able to stay on top. He was too tired now to give much thought to what he had done. He only knew that he had had his choice of remaining in the water alone or being pulled by the Black. If he was to die, he would rather die with the mighty stallion than alone. He took one last look behind and saw the *Drake* sink into the depths.

For hours Alec battled the waves. He had tied the rope

securely around his waist. He could hardly hold his head up. Suddenly he felt the rope slacken. The Black had stopped swimming! Alec anxiously waited; peering into the darkness he could just make out the head of the stallion. The Black's whistle pierced the air! After a few minutes, the rope became taut again. The horse had changed his direction. Another hour passed, then the storm diminished to high, rolling swells. The first streaks of dawn appeared on the horizon.

The Black had stopped four times during the night, and each time he had altered his course. Alec wondered whether the stallion's wild instinct was leading him to land. The sun rose and shone down brightly on the boy's head; the salt water he had swallowed during the night made him sick to his stomach. But when Alec felt that he could hold out no longer, he looked at the struggling, fighting animal in front of him, and new courage came to him.

Suddenly he realized that they were going with the waves, instead of against them. He shook his head, trying to clear his mind. Yes, they were riding in; they must be approaching land! Eagerly he strained his salt-filled eyes and looked into the distance. And then he saw it—about a quarter of a mile away was a small island, not much more than a sandy reef in the sea. But he might find food and water there, and have a chance to survive. Faster and faster they approached the white sand. They were in the breakers. The Black's scream shattered the stillness. He was able to walk; he staggered a little and shook his black head. Then his action shifted marvelously, and he went faster through the shallow water.

Alec's head whirled as he was pulled toward the beach

with ever-increasing speed. Suddenly he realized the danger of his position. He must untie this rope from around his waist, or else he would be dragged to death over the sand! Desperately his fingers flew to the knot; it was tight, he had made sure of that. Frantically he worked on it as the shore drew closer and closer.

The Black was now on the beach. Thunder began to roll from beneath his hoofs as he broke out of the water. Hours in the water had swelled the knot—Alec couldn't untie it! Then he remembered his pocketknife. Could it still be there? Alec's hand darted to his rear pants pocket. His fingers reached inside and came out with the knife.

He was now on the beach being dragged by the stallion; the sand flew in his face. Quickly he opened the knife and began to cut the rope. His body burned from the sand, his clothes were being torn off of him! His speed was increasing every second! Madly he sawed away at the rope. With one final thrust he was through! His outflung hands caressed the sand. As he closed his eyes, his parched lips murmured, "Yes—Uncle Ralph—it did—come in handy."

The Island

3

Alec opened his eyes. The sun, high in the heavens, beat down upon his bare head. His face felt hot, his tongue swollen. Slowly he pushed his tired body from the ground and then fell back upon the sand. He lay still a few moments. Then he gathered himself and once again attempted to rise. Wearily he got to his knees, then to his feet. His legs trembled beneath him. He unbuckled the battered life jacket and let it fall to the ground.

He looked around; he needed water desperately. He saw the Black's hoof marks in the sand. Perhaps, if he followed them, they would lead him to fresh water; he was sure that the stallion was as thirsty as he. Alec stumbled along. The hoof marks turned abruptly away from the ocean toward the interior of the island. There was no sign of vegetation around him—only hot sand. He turned and looked back at the now calm and peaceful sea. So much had happened in such a short space of time!

What had happened to the others? Was he the only one who had survived?

A few minutes later he turned and made his way up a high sand dune. At the crest he stopped. From where he stood he could see the entire island; it was small—not more than two miles in circumference. It seemed barren except for a few trees, bushes and scattered patches of burned grass. High rock cliffs dropped down to the sea on the other side of the island.

The Black's hoof marks led down the hill, and a short distance away beneath a few scattered trees, Alec saw a small spring-water pool. His swollen tongue ran across cracked lips as he stumbled forward. To the right of the spring, a hundred yards away, he saw the Black—hungrily feasting upon the dry grass. Alec again saw that small Arabian port and the crowd gathered around the prone figure of the Arab whom the Black had struck. Would he be safe from the stallion?

The Black looked up from his grazing. The boy noticed that the horse had torn or slipped off his halter somehow. The wind whipped through his mane; his smooth black body was brilliant in the sun. He saw Alec, and his shrill whistle echoed through the air. He reared, his front legs striking out. Then he came down, and his right foreleg pawed into the dirt.

Alec looked around him. There was no place to seek cover. He was too weak to run, even if there was. His gaze returned to the stallion, fascinated by a creature so wild and so near. Here was the wildest of all wild animals—he had fought for everything he had ever needed, for food, for leadership, for life itself; it was his nature to kill or be killed. The horse reared again; then he snorted and plunged straight for the boy.

Alec didn't move. His body was numb. Hypnotized, he watched the stallion coming. Then, twenty-five yards from him, the Black stopped. The whites of his eyes gleamed, his nostrils curled, his ears were back flat against his head. He whistled shrill, clear and long. Suddenly he moved between Alec and the spring. He pawed furiously at the earth.

Alec stood still, not daring to move. After what seemed hours, the stallion stopped tearing up the earth. His gaze turned from the boy to the pool and then back again. He whistled, half-reared, and then broke into his long stride, running back in the direction from which he had come.

Alec forced his legs into action, reached the spring and threw himself on the ground beside it. He let his face fall into the cool, clear water. It seemed that he would never get enough; he doused his head, and let the water run down his back. Then he tore off part of his shirt and bathed his skinned body. Refreshed, he crawled beneath the shaded bushes growing beside the pool. He stretched out, closed his eyes and fell asleep, exhausted.

Only once during the night did Alec stir; sleepily he opened his eyes. He could see the moon through the bushes, high above the star-studded sky. A big, black figure moved by the spring—the Black, and only a few feet away! He drank deeply and then raised his beautiful head, his ears pricked forward; he turned and trotted away.

Alec awoke very hungry the next morning. He had gone a day and a half without eating! He rose and drank from the spring. The next thing was to find food. He walked for quite some distance before he found anything edible. It was a berry bush; the fruit was unlike that of anything he had ever tasted before. But he might not easily find anything else that he could eat, so he made a meal of berries.

Then he explored the island. He found it to be flat between the sand dune that he had climbed the day before and the rocky cliffs of the other side of the island. He made no attempt to climb over the large boulders. There were few berry bushes and little grass, and Alec realized that food would be scarce for him and the Black. The island seemed to be totally uninhabited. He had seen no birds or animals of any kind.

He walked slowly back in the direction of the spring. From the top of the hill he looked out upon the open sea, hoping desperately that he would see a boat. Only the vast expanse of blue water spread before him. Below he saw the Black cantering along the beach. Alec forgot his problems in the beauty of the stallion as he swept along, graceful in his swift stride, his black mane and tail flying. When the horse vanished around the bend of the island, Alec walked down to the beach.

The next thing that he must do was to erect some sort of a shelter for himself; and first he must find driftwood. Alec's eyes swept the shore. He saw one piece, then another.

For the next few hours he struggled with the wood that he found cast upon the beach, dragging it back toward the spring. He piled it up and was surprised to see how much he had gathered. He looked for a long, heavy piece and found one that suited his purpose. He pulled it toward two adjoining scrub trees and hoisted it between the two crotches. Suddenly his arms shook and he stopped. Painted on the gray board was the name DRAKE—it had been part of one of the lifeboats! Alec stood still a moment, then grimly he fixed the plank securely in place.

Next he leaned the remaining pieces of wood on each side of the plank, making a shelter in the form of a tent. He filled in the open ends as well as he could. With his knife he skinned the bark from a tree and tied the pieces of wood together.

Alec went back to the beach and gathered all the seaweed that he could carry. He stuffed this into all the open holes. He surveyed his finished shelter—he was afraid a good wind would blow it down on top of him!

He looked up at the hot sun and guessed it to be near noon. His skin and clothes were wet with perspiration from the terrific heat. He cut a long, slender staff from a tree, tested it and found it to be strong. Carefully he skinned it and cut it the right length. Then he tied his knife securely to the end of the stick with a piece of bark.

A short time later Alec stood beside a small cove which he had discovered that morning. The water was clear and the sand glistened white beneath it. He seated himself upon the bank and peered eagerly into the water. He had read of people catching fish this way. After some time he saw a ripple. Carefully he raised his improvised spear. Then Alec flung it with all his might; the long stick whizzed down into the water and pierced its way into the white sand. He had missed!

He pulled his spear out and moved to another spot. Again he waited patiently. It was a long time before he saw another fish. A long slender shape moved in the shallow water beneath him. He raised his spear, took aim and plunged again. He saw the knife hit! Fearing the knife would slip out of the fish if he pulled the spear up, he jumped into the shallow water and shoved it against the bottom. Desperately Alec's arm flew down the stick, seeking the fish. The water was churned with sand. He came to the end, only the steel blade met his searching fingers. He had lost it!

For the rest of the afternoon, Alec strove to catch a fish. As darkness fell, he rose wearily to his feet and walked slowly back to his new "home." His eyes ached from the hours of strain of constant searching into the depths of the water.

On his way, he stopped at the berry bush and ate hungrily. When he reached the spring, he saw the Black not far away. He looked up, saw the boy and continued to eat. Moving from one place to another, he tore away at the small patches of grass that he could find. "I'll bet he's as hungry as I am," thought Alec. He dropped down and drank from the spring.

Darkness came rapidly. Suddenly Alec felt the stillness of the island—no birds, no animals, no sounds. It was as if he and the Black were the only living creatures in the world. Millions of stars shone overhead and seemed so close. The moon rose high and round; its reflection cast upon the pool.

The Black looked up from his grazing. He, too, seemed to watch the moon. Alec whistled—low, then louder and fading. A moment of silence. Then the stallion's shrill whistle pierced the night. Alec saw the Black look in his direction and then continue searching for grass. He smiled and crawled into his shelter. The day's work had made him tired and he was soon asleep.

The next morning found Alec beside the cove again with his spear, determined to catch a fish for breakfast. At noon he ate berries. Mid-afternoon he was sick; his head whirled and he could hardly keep his eyes from closing.

A small whirlpool appeared on the surface of the water. Alec grabbed the spear beside him and rose to his knees. He saw a gray shape in the water below. He raised his spear and moved it along with the fish. Then he plunged it! The spear quivered in its flight. He had hit! He jumped into the water, shoving the spear and fish against the bottom. He mustn't lose this one! His hand reached the knife. The fish was there—wriggling, fighting. Then he had it. Quickly he raised the fish from the water and threw it, and the spear, onto the bank. Wearily he climbed up and looked at his catch. "Two feet if it's an inch," he said hungrily. He drew out the spear, picked up the fish and went back to camp.

Alec washed the fish in the spring. Then he placed it upon a piece of wood and scaled it. Now if he could only get a fire started. He remembered watching a man in India build a fire without matches. Perhaps he could do the same.

He gathered some small pieces of bark, dry wood and a deserted bird's nest, and spread them on the ground in front of him. He picked out the driest piece of wood and, with his knife, bored a hole halfway through it. Carefully he tore small threads of straw from the bird's nest and placed them inside the hole; they would ignite quickly. Next he cut a sturdy elastic branch about eighteen inches long from a nearby tree, skinned it and placed one end in the hole. He leaned on the stick, bending it, and then rapidly turned the curved part like a carpenter's bit.

It seemed to Alec that an hour passed before a small column of smoke crept out of the hole. His tired arms pushed harder. Slowly a small flame grew and then the dry wood was on fire. He added more wood. Then he snatched the fish, wrapped it in some seaweed which he had previously washed, and placed it on top of the fire.

Later, Alec removed the fish. He tried a piece and found it to be good. Famished, he tore into the rest of it.

The days passed and the boy strove desperately to find food to keep himself alive; he caught only one more fish—it would be impossible for him to depend upon the sea for his living. He turned again to the berries, but they were fast diminishing. He managed to keep his fire going as the heat made dry fuel plentiful. However, that was of little use to him as he had nothing to cook.

One day as Alec walked along the beach, he saw a large red shell in the distance. He gripped his spear tighter; it looked like a turtle. Then hunger made him lose all caution and he rushed forward, his spear raised. He threw himself upon the shell, his knife digging into the opening where he believed the turtle's head to be. Desperately he turned the huge shell over—it was empty, cleaned out; only the hollow shell met Alec's famished gaze. He stood still, dazed. Then slowly he turned and walked back to camp.

The Black was drinking from the spring. His large body too was beginning to show signs of starvation. Alec no longer felt any fear of him. The stallion raised his proud head and looked at the boy. Then he turned and trotted off. His mane, long and flowing, whipped in the wind. His whistle filled the air.

Alec watched him, envying his proud, wild spirit. The horse was used to the hardships of the desert; probably he would outlive him. The boy's subconscious thought rose to the surface of his mind: "There's food, Alec, food—if you could only find some way of killing him!"

Then he shook his head, hating himself. Kill the animal that had saved his life? Never—even if he could, he would die of starvation first! The stallion reached the top of the hill and stood there, like a beautiful black statue, his gaze upon the open sea.

One morning Alec made his way weakly toward the rocky side of the island. He came to the huge rocks and climbed on top of one of them. It was more barren than any other part of the island. It was low tide and Alec's eyes wandered over the stony shore, looking for any kind of shellfish he might be able to eat. He noticed the mosslike substance on all the rocks at the water's edge, and on those that extended out. What was that stuff the biology teacher had made them eat last term in one of their experiments? Hadn't he called it *carragheen?* Yes, that was it. A sort of seaweed, he had said, that grew abundantly along the rocky parts of the Atlantic coast of Europe and North America. When washed and dried, it was edible for humans and livestock. Could the moss on the rocks below be it? Alec scarcely dared to hope.

Slowly Alec made the dangerous descent. He reached the water level and scrambled across the rocks. He took a handful of the soft greenish-yellow moss which covered them and raised it to his lips. It smelled the same. He tasted it. The moss was terribly salty from the sea, but it was the same as he had eaten that day in the classroom!

Eagerly he filled his pockets with it, then removed his shirt and filled it full. He climbed up again and hurried back to camp. There he emptied the moss onto the ground beside the spring. The next quarter of an hour he spent washing it, and then placed it out in the sun to dry.

Hungrily he tasted it again. It was better—and it was food!

When he had finished eating, the sun was falling into the ocean, and the skies were rapidly growing dark. In the distance Alec saw the stallion coming toward the spring. Quickly he picked up some of the moss for himself and left the rest on the ground beside the pool. Would the Black eat it? Alec hurried to his shelter and stood still watching intently.

The stallion rushed up, shook his long neck and buried his mouth into the water. He drank long. When he had finished he looked toward the boy, then his pink nostrils quivered. The Black put his nose to the ground and walked toward the moss which Alec had left. He sniffed at it. Then he picked a little up and started eating. He chewed long and carefully. He reached down for more.

That night Alec slept better than he had since he had been on the island. He had found food—food to sustain him and the Black!

The Wildest of All Wild Creatures

4

The next day Alec set out to obtain more of the carragheen. As he neared the rocks, he saw the stallion standing silently beside a huge boulder. Not a muscle twitched in his black body—it was as if an artist had painted the Black on white stone.

Alec climbed down into a small hollow and paused to look out over the rocks below. Suddenly he heard the stallion's scream, more piercing, more blood-curdling than he had ever heard it before. He looked up.

The Black was on his hind legs, his teeth bared. Then with a mighty leap, he shot away from the boulder toward Alec. Swiftly he came—faster with every magnificent stride. He was almost on top of him when he thundered to a halt and reared again. Alec jumped to the side, tripped on a stone and fell to the ground. High above him the Black's legs pawed the air, and then descended three yards in front of him! Again he went up and down—again and again he pounded. The ground on which Alec lay shook from the force of his hoofs. The stallion's eyes never left the ground in front of him.

Gradually his pounding lessened and then stopped. He raised his head high and his whistle shrilled through the air. He shook his head and slowly moved away, his nostrils trembling.

Alec regained his feet and cautiously made his way toward the torn earth, his brain flooded with confusion. There in front of him he saw the strewn parts of a long, yellowish-black body, and the venomous head of a snake, crushed and lifeless. He stood still—the suddenness of discovering life, other than the Black and himself on the island, astounding him! Sweat broke out on his forehead as he realized what a poisonous snake bite would have meant—suffering and perhaps death! Dazed, he looked at the stallion just a few feet away. Had the Black killed the snake to save him? Was the stallion beginning to understand that they needed each other to survive?

Slowly the boy walked toward the Black. The stallion's mane swept in the wind, his muscles twitched, his eyes moved restlessly, but he stood his ground as the boy approached. Alec wanted the horse to understand that he would not hurt him. Cautiously he reached a hand toward the stallion's head. The Black drew it back as far as he could without moving. Alec stepped closer and to the side of him. Gently he touched him for an instant. The stallion did not move. Again Alec attempted to touch the savage head. The Black reared and shook a little. Alec said soothingly, "Steady, Black fellow, I wouldn't hurt you." The stallion quivered, then reared again and broke. One hundred yards away he suddenly stopped and turned.

Alec gazed at him, standing there so still—his head raised high in the air. "We'll get out of this somehow, Black—working together," he said determinedly.

Alec walked back to the top of the rocks and again began his descent. He made his way carefully down to the water level. Cautiously he looked before he stepped—where there was one snake there might be more. Reaching the bottom, he once again filled his shirt full of the moss and made his way back. High above him he could see the Black looking out over the cliffs, his mane whipping in the wind. When he reached the top the stallion was still there. He followed a short distance behind as Alec went back to the spring.

Days passed and gradually the friendship between the boy and the Black grew. The stallion now came at his call and let Alec stroke him while he grazed. One night Alec sat within the warm glow of the fire and watched the stallion munching on the carragheen beside the pool. He wondered if the stallion was as tired of the carragheen as he. Alec had found that if he boiled it in the turtle shell it formed a gelatinous substance which tasted a little better than the raw moss. A fish was now a rare delicacy to him.

The flame's shadows reached out and cast eerie ghost-like patterns on the Black's body. Alec's face became grim as thoughts rushed through his brain. Should he try it tomorrow? Did he dare attempt to ride the Black? Should he wait a few more days? Go ahead—tomorrow. *Don't do it!* Go ahead——

The fire burned low, then smoldered. Yet Alec sat beside the fire, his eyes fixed on that blacker-than-night figure beside the spring.

The next morning he woke from a fitful slumber to find the sun high above. Hurriedly he ate some of the carragheen. Then he looked for the Black, but he was not in sight. Alec whistled, but no answer came. He walked toward the hill. The sun blazed down and the sweat ran from his body. If it would only rain! The last week had been like an oven on the island.

When he reached the top of the hill, he saw the Black at one end of the beach. Again he whistled, and this time there was an answering whistle as the stallion turned his head. Alec walked up the beach toward him.

The Black stood still as he approached. He went cautiously up to him and placed a hand on his neck. "Steady," he murmured, as the warm skin quivered slightly beneath his hand. The stallion showed neither fear nor hate of him; his large eyes were still turned toward the sea.

For a moment Alec stood with his hand on the Black's neck. Then he walked toward a sand dune a short distance away. The stallion followed. He stepped up the side of the dune, his left hand in the horse's thick mane. The Black's ears pricked forward, his eyes followed the boy nervously—some of the savageness returned to them, his muscles twitched. For a moment Alec was undecided what to do. Then his hands gripped the mane tighter and he threw himself on the Black's back. For a second the stallion stood motionless, then he snorted and plunged; the sand went flying as he doubled in the air. Alec felt the mighty muscles heave, then he was flung through the air, landing heavily on his back. Everything went dark.

Alec regained consciousness to find something warm against his cheek. Slowly he opened his eyes. The stallion was pushing him with his head. Alec tried moving his arms and legs, and found them bruised but not broken.

Wearily he got to his feet. The wildness and savageness had once more disappeared in the Black; he looked as though nothing had happened.

Alec waited for a few minutes—then once again led the stallion to the sand dune. His hand grasped the horse's mane. But this time he laid only the upper part of his body on the stallion's back, while he talked soothingly into his ear. The Black flirted his ears back and forth, as he glanced backward with his dark eyes.

"See, I'm not going to hurt you," Alec murmured, knowing it was he who might be hurt. After a few minutes, Alec cautiously slid onto his back. Once again, the stallion snorted and sent the boy flying through the air.

Alec picked himself up from the ground—slower this time. But when he had rested, he whistled for the Black again. The stallion moved toward him. Alec determinedly stepped on the sand dune and once again let the Black feel his weight. Gently he spoke into a large ear, "It's me. I'm not much to carry." He slid onto the stallion's back. One arm slipped around the Black's neck as he half-reared. Then like a shot from a gun, the Black broke down the beach. His action shifted, and his huge strides seemed to make him fly through the air.

Alec clung to the stallion's mane for his life. The wind screamed by and he couldn't see! Suddenly the Black swerved and headed up the sand dune; he reached the top and then down. The spring was a blur as they whipped by. To the rocks he raced, and then the stallion made a wide circle—his speed never diminishing. Down through a long ravine he rushed. Alec's blurred vision made out a black object in front of them, and as a flash he remembered the deep gully that was there. He felt the stallion gather himself; instinctively he leaned forward and held the Black firm and steady with his hands and knees. Then they were in the air, sailing over the black hole. Alec almost lost his balance when they landed but recovered himself in time to keep from falling off! Once again the stallion reached the beach, his hoofbeats regular and rhythmic on the white sand.

The jump had helped greatly in clearing Alec's mind. He leaned closer to the stallion's ear and kept repeating, "Easy, Black. Easy." The stallion seemed to glide over the sand and then his speed began to lessen. Alec kept talking to him. Slower and slower ran the Black. Gradually he came to a stop. The boy released his grip from the stallion's mane and his arms encircled the Black's neck. He was weak with exhaustion—in no condition for such a ride! Wearily he slipped to the ground. Never had he dreamed a horse could run so fast! The stallion looked at him, his head held high, his large body only slightly covered with sweat.

That night Alec lay wide awake, his body aching with pain, but his heart pounding with excitement. He had ridden the Black! He had conquered this wild, unbroken stallion with kindness. He felt sure that from that day on the Black was his—his alone! But for what—would they ever be rescued? Would he ever see his home again? Alec shook his head. He had promised himself he wouldn't think of that any more.

The next day he mounted the Black again. The horse half-reared but didn't fight him. Alec spoke softly in his ear, and the Black stood still. Then Alec touched him lightly on the side, and he walked—a long, loping stride. Far up the beach they went, then Alec tried to turn him by shifting his weight, and gently pushing the stallion's

head. Gradually the horse turned. Alec took a firmer grip
on his long mane and pressed his knees tighter against
the large body. The stallion broke out of his walk into a
fast canter. The wind blew his mane back into the boy's
face. The stallion's stride was effortless, and Alec found
it easy to ride. Halfway down the beach, he managed to
bring him back again to a walk, then to a complete stop.
Slowly he turned him to the right, then to the left, and
then around in a circle.

Long but exciting hours passed as Alec tried to make
the Black understand what he wanted him to do. The sun
was going down rapidly when he walked the stallion to the
end of the beach. The Black turned and stood still; a mile
of smooth, white sand stretched before them.

Suddenly the stallion bolted, almost throwing Alec to
the ground. He picked up speed with amazing swiftness.
Faster and faster he went. Alec hung low over his neck,
his breath coming in gasps. Down the beach the stallion
thundered. Tears from the wind rolled down Alec's
cheeks. Three-quarters of the way, he tried to check the
Black's speed. He pulled back on the flowing mane.
"Whoa, Black," he yelled, but his words were whipped
away in the wind.

Swiftly the stallion neared the end of the beach, and
Alec thought that his breathtaking ride of yesterday was
to be repeated. He pulled back harder on the mane.
Suddenly the Black's pace lessened. Alec flung one arm
around the stallion's neck. The Black shifted into his fast
trot, which gradually became slower and slower, until
Alec had him under control. Overjoyed he turned him,
and rode him over the hill to the spring. Together they
drank the cool, refreshing water.

With the days that followed, Alec's mastery over the

Black grew greater and greater. He could do almost anything with him. The savage fury of the unbroken stallion disappeared when he saw the boy. Alec rode him around the island and raced him down the beach, marveling at the giant strides and the terrific speed. Without realizing it, Alec was improving his horsemanship until he had reached the point where he was almost a part of the Black as they tore along.

One night Alec sat beside his campfire and stared into the flames that reached hungrily into the air; his knees were crossed and his elbows rested heavily upon them, his chin was cupped in his two hands. He was deep in thought. The *Drake* had left Bombay on a Saturday, the fifteenth of August. The shipwreck had happened a little over two weeks later, perhaps on the second of September. He had been on the island exactly—nineteen days. That would make it approximately the twenty-first of September. By now his family must think him dead! He doubled his fists. He had to find a way out; a ship just had to pass the island sometime. Daily he had stood on top of the hill peering out to sea, frantically hoping to sight a boat.

For the first time, Alec thought of the approaching cold weather. The heat had been so intense upon the island since his arrival that it had never entered his mind that it would soon get cold. Would his shelter offer him enough protection? He had used every available piece of wood on the island to reinforce it, but would that be enough? How cold would it get? Alec looked up at the clear, starlit sky.

He rose to his feet and walked toward the hill. The Black, standing beside the spring, raised his head and whistled when he saw him. He followed Alec as he climbed to the top. The boy's eyes swept the dark, rolling sea. White-crested swells rushed in and rolled up the beach. The stallion, too, seemed to be watching—his eyes staring into the night, his ears pricking forward. An hour passed, then they turned and made their way back to camp.

A wind started blowing from out of the west. Alec stoked the fire for the night, then crawled wearily into his shelter. He was tired, for he had spent most of the day gathering carragheen. He stretched out and was soon asleep.

He didn't know how long he had been sleeping, but suddenly the Black's shrill scream awakened him. Sleepily he opened his eyes; the air had grown hot. Then he heard a crackling noise above; his head jerked upward. The top of the shelter was on fire! Flames were creeping down the sides. Alec leaped to his feet and rushed outside.

A gale was sweeping the island and instantly he realized what had happened. Sparks from his campfire had been blown upon the top of the shelter and had easily set fire to the dry wood. He grabbed the turtle shell and ran to the spring. Filling it, he ran back and threw the water on the flames.

The Black pranced nervously beside the spring, his nostrils quivering, while Alec rushed back and forth with his little turtle shell full of water, trying to keep the fire from spreading. But it had a good start and soon it had enveloped the whole shelter. Smoke filled the air. The boy and the horse were forced to move farther and farther back.

Soon the two nearby trees caught. Alec knew that the fire could not spread much farther—the island was too barren of any real fuel. But right now the flames were devouring everything in sight. They roared and reached high into the air. There was nothing that Alec could do. The one thing he really needed—his shelter—was gone. And there was no more wood.

The fire burned a long time before it started to die down. Then the wind too began to diminish. Alec sat beside the spring, watching the flames, until the first streaks of dawn appeared in the sky. He blinked his smoke-filled eyes, gritted his teeth—he wasn't licked yet! He'd find some way to make a shelter, and if that wasn't possible, then he'd sleep outside like the Black.

Determinedly he set out for the beach. Perhaps some wood had been swept ashore during the night. The Black trotted ahead of him. Then Alec saw him snort and rear as he reached the top of the hill, and plunge back down again. Alec hurried forward. From the crest of the hill, he looked down. Below him was a ship anchored four hundred yards off the island!

He heard voices. He saw a rowboat being drawn up on the beach by five men. Incredulous, unable to shout, he rushed down the hill.

"You were right, Pat, there *is* someone on this island!" he heard one of the men shout to the other.

And the other replied in a thick Irish brogue, "Sure, and I knew I saw a fire reaching into the heavens!"

Rescue

5

Alec's eyes blurred; he couldn't see. He stumbled and fell and then clambered to his feet. Again he rushed forward. Then they had their arms around him.

"For the love of St. Patrick," the man called Pat groaned, "he's just a boy!"

Words jumbled together and stuck in Alec's throat as he looked into the five pairs of eyes staring at him. Then he found his voice. "We're saved!" he yelled. "We're saved, Black, we're saved!"

The sailors looked at him—he was a strange sight! His red hair was long and disheveled, his face and body so brown that they would have taken him for a native had it not been for the torn remnants of his clothing, which hung loosely on him.

One of the men stepped forward. From his uniform he was obviously the captain of the ship. "Everything is going to be all right, son," he said as he placed an arm around Alec and steadied him.

Slowly Alec gained control of himself. "I'm okay now, sir," he said.

The sailors gathered around him. "Is there someone else with you on this island?" the captain asked.

"Only the Black, sir."

The men looked at one another, and then the captain spoke again, "Who's the Black, son?" he asked.

"He's a horse, sir," Alec answered.

And then he told them his story—of the storm and the shipwreck, the hours spent in the raging sea holding desperately to the rope tied to the stallion's neck, their fight against starvation on the island, his conquest of the Black, and the fire which that night had reduced his shelter to ashes. Sweat broke out on his forehead as he once again lived through the twenty days of hardships and suffering since the *Drake* had gone down.

When he had finished there was a moment of silence, and then one of the men spoke. "This lad is imagining things, Captain. What he needs is some hot food and a good bed!"

Alec looked from one face to another and saw that they didn't believe him. Rage filled him. Why should they be so stupid? Was his story so fantastic? He'd prove it to them, then—he'd call the Black.

He raised his fingers to his lips and whistled. "Listen," he shouted. "Listen!" The men stood still. A minute passed, and then another—only the waves lapping on the beach could be heard in the terrifying stillness of the island.

Then the captain's voice came to him, "We have to go

now, son. We're off our course and away behind schedule.''

Dazed, Alec's eyes turned from the island to the freighter lying at anchor, smoke belching from its two stacks. It was larger than the *Drake*.

The captain's voice again broke through his thoughts. "We're bound for South America—Rio de Janeiro is our first stop. We can take you there and radio your parents from the ship that you're alive!"

The captain and Pat had him by the arms; the others were in the boat ready to shove off. Desperately Alec tried to collect his thoughts. He was leaving the island. He was leaving the Black. The Black—who had saved his life! He jerked himself free, he was running up the beach.

Their mouths wide open, the sailors watched him as he stumbled up the hill. They saw him reach the top and raise his fingers to his lips. His whistle reached them— then there was silence.

Suddenly, an inhuman scream shattered the stillness—a wild, terrifying call! Stunned, they stood still and the hairs on the back of their necks seemed to curl. Then as if by magic, a giant black horse, his mane waving like flame, appeared beside the boy. The horse screamed again, his head raised high, his ears pricked forward. Even at this distance they could see that he was a tremendous horse—a wild stallion.

Alec flung his arms around the Black's neck and buried his head in the long mane. "We're leaving together, Black—together," he said. Soothingly he talked to the stallion, steadying him. After a few minutes he descended the hill and the horse hesitatingly followed. He reared as they approached the sailors, his legs pawing in the air.

The men scrambled into the boat; only Pat and the captain stood their ground. Fearfully they watched the Black as he strode toward them. He drew back; his black eyes glanced nervously from Alec to the group of men. Alec patted him, coaxed him. His action was beautiful, and every few steps he would jump swiftly to one side.

Approximately thirty yards away, Alec came to a halt. "You just have to take us both, Captain! I can't leave him!" he yelled.

"He's too wild. We couldn't take him, we couldn't handle him!" came the answer.

"I can handle him. Look at him now!"

The Black was still, his head turned toward the freighter as if he understood what actually was going on. Alec's arm was around his neck. "He saved my life, Captain. I can't leave him here alone. He'll die!"

The captain turned, spoke with the men in the boat. Then he shouted, "There isn't any possible way of getting that devil on board!" He paused. "How're you going to get him out there?" The captain pointed to the ship.

"He can swim," answered Alec. "He'll follow me. I know he will."

There was another discussion between captain and crew. When he turned, the captain's heavily lined face was more grim than ever. He doffed his cap and ran a large hand through his gray hair. "Okay, son," he said, "you win—but you'll have to get him out there!"

Alec's heart beat heavily and he gazed at the stallion. 'Come on, Black," he said. He walked forward a few steps. The Black hesitated and then followed. Again Alec moved ahead. Slowly they approached the group. Then the Black halted, his nostrils quivered and he reared.

"Get in the boat, Captain," Alec shouted. "Move up to the bow. I'm going to get in the stern when you get her in the water."

The captain ordered his men to shove off, and he and Pat climbed in; then they waited for Alec.

Alec turned to the Black. "This is our chance, Black," he said. "Come on!" He could see the stallion was nervous; the horse had learned to trust him, but his natural instincts still warned him against the others. Soothingly Alec spoke to him. Slowly he backed away— the Black raised his head nervously, then followed. As the boy neared the boat, the stallion stopped. Alec kept backing up and climbed into the boat. "Row slowly," he said, without turning his eyes away from the horse.

As they moved away from the beach Alec called, "Come on, Black!" The stallion pranced, his head and tail erect, his ears forward. He half-reared and then stepped into the water. Like a flash he was back on the beach; his foreleg pawing into the sand and sending it flying. His black eyes never left the boat as it moved slowly out into the water. He ran a short way down the beach, and then back again.

Alec realized the terrific fight that the stallion was waging with himself. He whistled. The Black stopped in his tracks and answered. Slowly the boat moved farther away.

Suddenly the stallion rose high into the air on his hind legs, and then plunged into the water. "Come on, Black," shouted Alec. "Swim!"

The Black was in water up to his big chest now—then he was swimming and coming swiftly toward the boat.

"Row for the ship, Captain," yelled Alec.

The black head rose in the water behind them, the eyes

fearfully following Alec as he half-hung out of the boat and called to the stallion. The large, black body slid through the water, its legs working like pistons.

Soon they reached the freighter. The captain and three men sprang up the ladder. Only Pat remained behind with Alec. "Keep him there for two minutes!" the captain yelled over his shoulder.

The Black reached the rowboat and Alec managed to get his hand on the stallion's head. "Good boy!" he murmured proudly. Then he heard the captain's hail from on top of the deck. He looked up and saw the cargo hoist being lowered; on the end was a wide belly band to go around the Black so that he could be lifted up. He had to get that band around the stallion's stomach!

Alec saw the Black's eyes leave him and gaze fearfully at the line descending over his head. Suddenly he swam away from the boat. Frantically Alec called to him.

As the band came within reach, Pat grabbed it—his fingers tore at the straps and buckles. "We've got to get this around him somehow!" he shouted to Alec. "It's the only way!"

Alec tried desperately to think. Certainly there must be some way! The stallion had turned and once again was looking in their direction. If he could only get close to him. "Let me have the band, Pat, and more line," he said.

Pat handed it to him and signaled above. "And what are you going to do?" he asked.

But Alec didn't seem to hear his query. He gripped the straps of the band tightly. "We've come this far," he said to himself. He climbed over the side and lowered himself into the water. Pat was too astonished to speak. Alec swam a few yards toward the Black, the band stretched out behind him; then he stopped and trod water. He called softly and the stallion swam toward him.

He came within an arm's reach and Alec touched him, keeping his body far enough away to avoid the driving legs. How could he get the band around the stallion? Pat was yelling suggestions, but Alec could think of only one way that might be successful.

He sank lower in the water, his hand gradually sliding down the Black's neck; he held the straps of the belt tightly in the other. He took a deep breath and filled his lungs with air; then he dived sideways and felt the waters close over his head. Down he went, striving desperately to get enough depth to clear the stallion's legs. He swam directly beneath the Black's belly; the water churned white above his head and he caught a glimpse of striking hoofs. When he felt sure that he was on the other side, he started up, his fingers still tightly closed upon the straps and the band dragging behind.

When he reached the surface, he found the stallion in the same position, his eyes searching for him. Now the band was directly below the Black! He signaled for Pat to pull up the slack between the boat and the horse. All that he had to do now was to tighten the band around the stallion by getting these straps through the buckles on the other side! Alec moved closer to the Black. He would have to take the chance of being kicked. He kept as close to the middle of the stallion as possible. Then he was beside him. He felt the waters swirling on both sides. The line was taut now, ascending in the air to the top of the hoist on the freighter.

The Black became uneasy. Alec reached over his back and desperately tried to pull the straps through the buckles. A searing pain went through his leg as one of the

Black's hoofs struck him. His leg went limp. Minutes passed as his fingers worked frantically. Then he had the straps through and began pulling the band tighter. The stallion went wild with rage as he felt it tighten around him. Alec pulled harder. Once again he felt the Black's hoof strike his leg—but there was no pain. He had the straps through the buckles as far as they would go; he made sure they were securely fastened, and then wearily pushed himself away from the Black.

A safe distance away, Alec signaled the men on the freighter to hoist. He heard the starting of a motor and the chain line became more taut. Then the stallion was dragged through the water until he was beside the ship; his teeth were bared, his eyes were filled with hate! Then the hoist started lifting him up. Slowly the Black moved out of the water—up, up in the air he ascended, his legs pawing madly!

Alec swam toward the rowboat, his leg hanging limp behind him. When he reached it, Pat hung over the side and helped him up into the boat. "Good boy," he said.

The pain in his leg made Alec's head whirl. Blackness seemed to be settling down upon him—he shook his head. Then he felt Pat's big arm around his waist and he went limp.

When Alec regained consciousness, he found himself in bed. Beside him sat Pat—a large grin on his face, his blue eyes crinkling in the corners. "For the love of St. Patrick," he exclaimed, "I thought you were going to sleep forever!"

"What time is it, Pat?" Alec asked. "Have I been sleeping long?"

Pat ran a large, gnarled hand through his black hair.

"Well, not so long, son—you were pretty tired, y'know."
He paused. "Let's see, we picked you up Tuesday
morning and now it's Wednesday night."

"Whew!" said Alec, "that's some sleeping!"

"Well, we did wake you up a couple of times to give
you some soup, but I guess you wouldn't be remembering
now."

Alec moved slightly and felt a pain go through his leg.
His eyes turned to Pat. "Did I get hurt bad?" he asked.

"The Doc says not—went to the bone, but it's healing
nicely. You'll be all right in a few days."

"And the Black—what happened?"

"Lad, never in my life did I ever expect to see the like
of him! What a fight he put up—he almost tore the boat
apart!" Pat's blue eyes flashed. "Lord, what a devil! The
moment his hoofs touched the deck he wanted to fight. If
we hadn't still had the band around him, he would have
killed us all! He plunged and struck his legs out like I've
never seen before. He wouldn't stand still. You could
have helped us, son. We hoisted him in the air again, off
his feet. I thought he had gone crazy, his face was
something terrible to see—and those screams, I'll hear
them to my dying day!"

Pat stopped and moved uneasily in his seat. Then he
continued, "It was when one of the boys got a little too
close, and that black devil struck him in the side and he
fell at our feet, that we decided there was nothing else to
do but choke him! We got our lassoes around his neck and
pulled until we had him pretty near gone. It was tough on
him, but there was no other way. When he was almost
unconscious, we let him down once again and somehow
managed to lower him below.

"It was a job, lad, that I hope I'll never have to be in on

again. We have some other horses and cattle in the hold, too, and they're all scared to death of him. It's a regular bedlam down there now, and I hate to think what might happen when that horse is himself again! We've got him in the strongest stall, but I'm wondering whether even that'll hold him!"

Pat rose from his chair and walked to the other side of the cabin.

Alec was silent, then he spoke slowly, "I'm sorry I've caused you all so much trouble. If only I'd been able to——"

"I didn't aim to make you feel like that, lad," Pat interrupted. "I guess we knew what we were doing, and from the looks of that animal he's worth it. Only we all realize now that he needs you to handle him—the Lord help anyone else that tries to!"

"Tell the captain I'll repay him and you fellows, too, Pat, somehow."

"Sure, lad, and now I have some work to do. You try and get some more sleep, and tomorrow or the next day you'll be on your feet again." He paused on his way to the door. "If you give me your address, we can radio your parents that you are safe, and tell them where we're bound."

Alec smiled and wrote his address on the piece of paper Pat handed him. "Tell them I'll be with them—soon," he said as he finished.

King of the Herd

6

A few days later Alec got out of bed for the first time. His injured leg weakly supported him. As he dressed, a knock came upon the door.

"Come in," he called.

Pat entered. In his hand was a radiogram. "It's from your folks." He grinned.

Alec took it, and read: "Thank God you're safe. Cabling money to Rio de Janeiro. Hurry home. Love. Mother and Dad."

He was silent a minute, then looked up at Pat. "It'll be great to get home," he said.

Pat smiled. "How's the leg feel?"

"Not so bad," Alec answered, as he continued his dressing. "How's the Black doing?"

"I'm afraid he's feeling better—it's a good thing you're able to get down there today!" answered Pat.

Alec drew on a pair of large pants which one of the sailors had given him.

"Kinda big for you, aren't they?" asked Pat.

"Better than walking around without any." Alec grinned.

He finished dressing and slowly limped to the door. "Have to get to the Black before he tears the place apart." He folded the radiogram and placed it carefully in his pocket. "Thanks, Pat," he said.

"Don't stay on your feet too long, son," Pat warned. "Remember what the Doc said."

When Alec entered the hold, he heard the Black's pounding above the bedlam of the other horses and cattle. He came to the horse's stall and saw his dark head raised above the door. His large eyes moved nervously about. Alec called—the stallion's head jerked toward him. His nostrils quivered and he neighed. Alec reached a hand out. "Hello, fella," he said, "did you miss me?" The stallion shook his head and thrust his nose toward him. Alec ran his hand across the soft muzzle.

He took from his pocket an apple which he had saved from his breakfast. He held it out to the Black, who swept it out of his hand. Alec picked up the currycomb and brush from the floor, opened the door and went inside. "Guess it was tough on you, fella, but they didn't have any choice," he said. The next hour he spent in brushing the Black until his body shone brilliantly.

The days passed quickly for Alec, as he spent most of his time in the hold with the Black. His leg healed and was soon as good as ever. The captain and Pat at first attempted to get him interested in the boat and the voyage, but at last they gave up. The friendship between the boy and the stallion was something too much for them to understand.

The captain's hand rose to his chin as he and Pat watched Alec inside the stall. "Y'know, Pat," he said, "it's almost uncanny the way those two get along—a wild beast like that, a killer, and yet gentle as a kitten when the boy's around."

Pat nodded. "Yes, sir," he said, "one of the strangest things I've ever seen. I wonder where it'll take them?"

Five days later they steamed into Rio de Janeiro. The captain delegated Pat to go with Alec to the wireless office, where he could secure the money his family had sent him, and help arrange for his sailing to the United States.

As Alec walked with Pat through the South American city, he thought how close he was getting to home. He was on the last leg of his journey! They reached the office and went in. Pat spoke to the man at the desk in Portuguese. After a few minutes the man handed him a pen, and Alec signed his name. Then he was handed his money.

Next they went to the ticket office. There they found that the next boat for the United States would sail the following day. Alec had just enough money for himself and the Black, and he booked passage. He looked at Pat. "That doesn't leave me anything for the captain and you fellows."

"Don't you worry about that, Alec," Pat answered.

When they returned to the boat, Alec made his way to the captain's office. He found him behind his large desk working over some papers in front of him. He looked up, motioned the boy to sit down and continued writing. Finally he stopped and sat back in his chair.

"Well, son," he said, "we've come to the parting of the ways, haven't we?"

"Yes, sir," answered Alec. "Pat and I got the money and everything all right." He shoved his hand in his pocket and drew out some change. "But this is all I have left. You see, sir—well, Mother and Dad didn't know about the Black, and what they sent was just enough to get us both back to New York."

"And now you're thinking about what you owe us, aren't you?" the captain interrupted.

"Yes, sir," replied Alec. "If it hadn't been for you, we'd probably still be back on the island."

The captain got up from his chair and walked over beside Alec. He placed an arm on his shoulder. "Don't you worry about us, son. We don't expect anything—and you and that horse gave us more excitement around here than we've had in years." He smiled, and they walked toward the door. "You just see that you get the rest of the way home safely, and that'll be fine!"

"Thanks, Captain," Alec said as he went out onto the deck.

"And don't let anyone steal that black devil from you either!"

"I won't, sir, and thanks again," replied Alec.

The next afternoon he walked the Black down the gangplank. He had a firm grip on the stallion's halter, and kept talking soothingly to him. The ship that was to take them home had arrived during the night and was now being loaded with cargo. Pat and some of the sailors gathered around him as he reached the dock.

One by one they said good-bye, until only Pat remained. "So long, Alec," he said. "Take good care of yourself."

"You bet," answered Alec. "And remember, Pat, whenever you get to New York, you promised to look us up."

"Sure, some day perhaps . . ." He paused. "What are you going to do with the Black when you get him home?"

"I don't know, Pat; I haven't given it much thought. I just hope Dad and Mother will let me keep him."

Pat was looking at the stallion. "He's built for speed. I'll bet he could tear up a track."

"You mean—race?" asked Alec.

"Perhaps. Eight years ago, before I went to sea, I trained some pretty good horses in Ireland. I've never seen any that looked more like a runner than this one!"

"You can bet your last penny on that," Alec said. Memories flashed back of his breathtaking rides on the island. "Well, Pat, I have to go now, they've almost finished loading over there. Good-bye." He held out his hand and the other grasped it.

"So long, Alec," he replied, "and good luck!"

"So long, Pat."

Alec led the Black to the other end of the dock. A group of horses were gathered in one corner waiting their turn to be loaded. Dockhands rushed back and forth. A mixture of cattle and fruit smells filled the air.

The Black reared, and the other horses shrilled in fright as they saw him. Alec took the stallion to a far corner. His ears were pitched forward, his eyes glared masterfully over the others.

"Reminds you of the old days, doesn't it, fella?" said Alec. He smiled, wondered what his mother and dad would say when they saw the Black. He was glad now they had moved out from the city last year to Flushing, one of New York's suburbs. He was sure he would be able to find a place near his home where he could keep the Black, providing his mother and dad would let him!

Suddenly the Black screamed loudly and Alec felt him tremble. An answering scream filled the air. The other horses shoved each other in confusion. Alec saw a chestnut stallion being led toward the dock. He was big, almost as big as the Black.

The men leading him stopped on the farther side of the dock. Alec was thankful that he wasn't going to be loaded on the same boat with the Black. The black stallion pulled restlessly at his rope, his head high in the air, his eyes never leaving the chestnut.

The man holding him was having his troubles, too. The chestnut rose in the air. The Black screamed and pulled harder on the rope. The other horses began to neigh loudly. Alec tried to quiet the Black, but he could see that something wild and instinctive was rising within him. He remembered the stories that his uncle had told him about the tribes of wild horses—how one stallion alone was king!

"Whoa, Boy—take it easy," he said. The stallion was snorting, one leg pawed into the wood, his ears were flat back against his head. The chestnut's whistle rose loud and clear. Alec saw him rise into the air. There were yells and shouts from the sailors. Then he saw the man holding the chestnut fall to the ground, and the stallion was loose!

The Black reared on his hind legs, and his scream was terrorizing. Alec knew now that he could not hold him. The rope was jerked from his hands.

The chestnut and the Black rushed toward each other, their thunderous hoofs shaking the boards. The distance between the two closed rapidly, and then they clashed! High in the air they rose on their hind legs, their forelegs, pawing, striking madly at each other. Teeth bared, they lunged at each other's throats. The Black got a hold on the chestnut and savagely hung on. Furiously they kicked, their manes whipping in the air. The chestnut broke the Black's hold, and for a minute they squared off; then they were lunging at each other again.

Alec couldn't look—couldn't look away. Sounds of hoofs striking bodies, and squeals of terror from the other horses mingled with the screams of the two savages who fought for supremacy. The Black shrieked—louder than Alec had ever heard him before. His strength and experience were slowly overpowering the chestnut. His striking hoofs swept the chestnut stallion off his feet, and he fell to the dock. The Black went high in the air and his hoofs came down on top of him. Alec closed his eyes. A moment later the Black's scream again came to his ears.

He saw the Black standing over the chestnut, his eyes blazing, his body streaked with blood and with lather. What would he do next?

The Black's head turned toward the group of horses gathered in the corner. Majestically he strode toward them. They neighed nervously, but none moved. Slowly the black stallion walked around them—his eyes piercing, triumphant.

Alec followed him. He heard voices yelling at him, "Keep away, boy, keep away till he calms down!" But he kept walking. The Black turned and saw him.

The stallion stopped still. Alec came closer. The huge black body was torn and bleeding, but his head was high, his mane flowing. Alec watched his eyes—he had learned much from the stallion's eyes. He saw a little of the wildness leave them. His nostrils stopped trembling. Alec spoke to him softly.

A minute passed, then another. He picked up the rope, still attached to the Black's halter. He drew up the slack and then pulled gently. The stallion's head turned toward him. He hesitated a moment, and then turned back to the other horses. Alec waited patiently while the stallion surveyed his newly acquired band. Then he looked again at Alec. It seemed to Alec as if he was trying to make up his mind between them. He took a few more steps toward the horses—then he turned and walked quietly toward the boy.

Shouts of astonishment broke out among the sailors. Alec attempted to lead the stallion toward the gangplank. The Black stopped and turned his head once again toward the horses. For a minute he gazed at them. The ship's whistle blew. Alec pulled a little harder. "Come on, Black," he said. Another minute passed, and then the stallion turned again.

The sailors fell away as they approached. When they reached the gangplank, Alec looked over his shoulder and saw a crowd gathering around the chestnut, who was slowly climbing to his feet. The man was running his hands over the horse's legs. Then he walked him—the chestnut seemed to be all right. Alec was glad—for even though the chestnut had started the fight, it might have meant staying behind if the Black had hurt him seriously.

Up the plank they went—onto the ship. One sailor, more courageous than the rest, called to Alec, "Follow me, kid—down this way!" He led the way to a box stall, and then moved a safe distance away.

Alec led the Black into the stall, took off the halter, and spread the bedding around. He filled a pail full of water. The sailor brought him the antiseptic he'd asked for. He was young, not much older than Alec, and his face was filled with wonder. "I never in my life saw anything like that," he said.

"Neither did I," answered Alec. He felt the Black's legs and sides. "It would be swell if you could get me some clean cloths," he said. "I have to be careful of these cuts."

"Sure thing!" the sailor answered. "We're shoving off in a few minutes, but I'll be back with 'em as soon as I can."

Home

7

Alec heard the ship's whistle give three short blasts. The last horse came into the hold, shying nervously as he passed the Black's stall. The stallion reached his great head out over the door, his ears pricked forward, and his eyes moving from stall to stall.

The boat trembled as the engines began to turn over. Alec bent down to wet the cloth in his hand. "It won't be long now," he thought. Carefully he cleaned a deep cut in the Black's side where the chestnut had kicked him. He felt the stallion quiver as the antiseptic entered the wound. He was so big and powerful. Would he prove too much for Alec to handle? And what *would* his mother and father say when they saw him? He had thought of a place to keep him. Two blocks from their house in Flushing was an old run-down estate. The large, brown house was now being used to accommodate tourists. But in the rear was an old barn, badly in need of repair, and an acre of ground. It would be an ideal place to stable the Black. If only his parents would let him keep the stallion, he would fix up the barn himself, and find work after school to pay for his feed.

Alec finished his work, and the Black turned his head. "Had a pretty tough day, haven't you, fella?" The stallion shook his head, and shoved his nose against the boy's chest, pushing him back against the wall. Alec laughed and picked up the pail and cloths.

He shut the door of the stall behind him. The stallion's nostrils quivered; his eyes followed Alec as he backed slowly away. "Take it easy now, Boy," he said. "I have to see what my own bunk looks like!"

The Black screamed as Alec began to climb the stairs. There was a loud crash as the stallion's hoofs went through the side of the stall. Alec rushed back. "Easy, Boy," he said. "Easy." The Black shoved his nose toward him, and he placed his hand upon the tender skin.

Grooms from the other stalls came running toward them. "Everything all right?" one asked.

"Yes," answered Alec. "He's still excited."

"He's a mean one, he is! You'll have to watch him!"

"He just doesn't like to be left alone," said Alec, "so I guess I'll stick around."

The grooms went back to their jobs. Alec looked at the stallion. "Black," he said, "you're something!" He went around to the side of the stall and pushed the broken board back into place. He looked around the hold, and noticed that the grooms had opened cots and were placing them beside the stalls. Alec found one and did the same. "Looks as though I'm going to bunk down here whether I like it or not," he said.

Alec tossed on his cot that night, as the ship plowed through heavy, pitching seas. Every wave seemed destined to send him rolling off his bed. The horses were finding it difficult, too, and their poundings made the hold a bedlam. Alec could hear the Black pawing at the floor of his stall.

It was still rough the next morning, and continued to be rough throughout the day. The horses began to get sick and the grooms were kept busy. Only the Black remained well. He still held his head as high as ever, and moved gingerly about in his stall.

Night fell and the ocean became wilder. Bolts of lightning flashed in the sky and a gale whistled outside. Alec thought of the *Drake* and the storm that had sent it down to the bottom. He rose from his cot and went to the stall door. The Black was awake, and pushed his nose toward the boy.

"Not frightened, are you, fella?" A streak of lightning made the hold as bright as day, and there was a loud crack as it struck the water. The ship quivered. Alec's fingers tightened on the Black's mane. Again darkness, and the ship lurched forward. The engines throbbed and once more took up their steady chant.

The Black's eyes were moving about restlessly. He shook his head and his foreleg pawed into the bedding of the stall. Alec couldn't blame him for being frightened. He reached in his pocket for some sugar and held it out to the stallion. The Black moved away and pounded harder than ever.

The ship staggered as a wave crashed against it. The grooms were rising from their cots, awakened by the storm. The other horses were quiet—most of them too sick to cause any trouble. Alec was afraid the Black would get out of control. He opened the door and went inside. The stallion backed into a corner. Alec held out the sugar. "Easy, Boy," he said. The Black's head was high in the air. He stopped his pounding as Alec put a hand on his neck. He reached down for the sugar. "That's a good fella!" said Alec. Slowly the Black quieted under his hand.

Hours passed and dawn broke in the sky. The wind lessened and a torrent of rain poured down. One of the grooms came over to the Black's stall. "Isn't he sick at all?" he asked.

"A little," Alec answered, "but mostly he's just nervous, though."

The man looked at the Black admiringly. "He certainly must have an iron constitution to go through seas like this without being sick. He's the only animal on board that isn't!"

Later in the day Alec began to feel queasy in his stomach. Desperately he fought against it. At last he had to admit that he was seasick. "Guess you're a better man than I am, Black," he said.

The next few days Alec didn't care whether he lived or died. Most of the grooms were sick, too, so they didn't pay much attention to him. The ship's first mate, who acted as doctor on the ship, came down, and tried to make him go to his cabin, but sick as he was, he realized that he couldn't leave the Black.

Three mornings later, Alec weakly rose to his feet and walked up to the stallion. The ship had stopped rolling. "Hello, Boy," he said. "I see you're as spry as ever!" The stallion's ears pricked forward and he shook his head.

A groom came up. "How d'you feel, kid?" he asked.

"A little weak," Alec said, "but otherwise okay." He paused. "How much longer before we reach New York?"

"About two more days," the groom answered, "unless we run into some more rough weather—but I think we've had our share of it."

"I hope so," Alec said—and he meant it.

Two days later the ship's whistle blew for Quarantine, where the boat was to be inspected before passing into New York harbor. The Quarantine inspectors entered the hold and went from stall to stall, examining the horses. Alec noticed that each groom produced papers and showed them to the officer in charge. What would he do when they came to him? Perhaps it would be better if he went over now and explained why he didn't have any. Alec started toward the officer. Suddenly the Black's scream stopped him in his tracks. He turned and saw that one of the inspectors had crossed the hold and was opening the stallion's door. "Watch out!" shouted Alec, but he was too late. The Black reared and struck out with his front feet, striking the man and sending him flying against the door.

Alec rushed to the stall and flung himself between the stallion and the inspector. Desperately he grabbed the halter. The Black's frightened eyes never left the man on the floor. The inspector, spluttering angrily, climbed to his feet. Alec felt relieved; if he was angry, he couldn't be hurt very badly. His trouser was ripped where the Black had struck him, but there were no other signs of injury.

The other inspectors came running. "What's the matter here?" asked the officer in charge.

"This horse attacked me, sir!" said the man. "He's a dangerous animal."

The officer walked closer to the door. "What have you to say about it?" he asked Alec, who was tightly holding the Black's halter.

Alec looked at the tall, sharp-featured man, and wondered whether the officer could prevent the Black from entering the country. He felt sick at the thought. They just couldn't do that. He met the officer's eyes. "I'm sorry about what happened, sir, and I know he wouldn't have done what he did if your inspector hadn't entered the stall like that. You see, he isn't used to people, sir. No one has ever been near him except me."

The officer's eyes traveled over the stallion. Then he walked toward the door and went inside. Alec took a firmer grip on the halter. "It's all right, Black," he said. "Whoa, Boy." The stallion moved uneasily.

The officer walked slowly around him. "He's quite a horse. Is he yours?" he asked.

"Yes, sir," answered Alec.

"Are your papers all in order?"

"I haven't any, sir, but the captain told me it would be all right. We were in a shipwreck and——"

"Oh, you're the one," interrupted the officer. "We've received orders about you. You're to go through." He smiled. "You've certainly had a tough enough trip as it is without our making it any tougher." He turned to the inspector, who had his trouser rolled up and was washing his leg. "How's the leg, Sandy?" he asked.

"It's okay, I guess, sir—but that horse is the wildest one I've seen around here in fourteen years!" he answered.

"And I think the best, too!" The officer smiled. He turned to Alec. "You must have quite a story, son—shipwrecked, and turning up with an animal like this."

"It is, sir. We were both on the *Drake* when it went down, and from what I've heard we're the only survivors." He paused. "It's a pretty long story, sir." He turned to the stallion. "How about it, fella?" The Black snorted.

With a clean bill of health, the ship left Quarantine and steamed through the Narrows into the harbor. Alec eagerly peered through the porthole beside the Black's stall. His throat tightened as the skyline rose before him. Here he was back home again! How differently he had left it five months ago—it seemed more like five years!

Alec felt the Black's heavy breathing on his arm. He turned and ran his hand across the tender nostrils. "Well, Black," he said, "we're home!"

He could see the two small tugs effortlessly pushing the big freighter. The buildings climbed higher and higher into the sky. A large liner, ocean-bound, passed them— its stacks belching white smoke into the heavens. Tankers and flatboats loaded with railroad cars crept past. In the distance Alec saw the Statue of Liberty. His eyes filled with tears. What was the matter with him? He was too old to become emotional. But his throat tightened and he swallowed hard as they neared the symbol of freedom and home!

An electric ferry plowed through the water beside the ship, its decks crowded with people. The sun was sinking behind the buildings on the Jersey shore. The Black sniffed at Alec's hand. He turned and smiled. "Only a few more minutes, Black," he said. He reached in his pocket and pulled out two lumps of sugar and a radiogram. The stallion took the sugar from his hand. Alec opened the yellow piece of paper, and read it once again: "Will be at pier. Can hardly wait. Love. Mother and Dad."

The steamer was now opposite Brooklyn, where it was to dock. The tugboats swung the ship around and headed toward the shore. The hold was filled with noise as the crew prepared to unload the ship. The Black became uneasy.

Then the boat slid up beside the dock. Alec heard the bumping of the boat against the dock. A few minutes later the hold doors were thrown open.

The crew began to unload the horses. Because of the Black's reputation, they made him wait until all the others were off. Then one of the crew signaled to him. "Okay," he said. Alec smiled as he saw him move quickly away out of the way.

Alec led the Black out of his stall, his hand tight on the lead rope. The stallion's head rose high; he knew that something unusual was going to happen. Lightly he pranced toward the door. The pier was crowded with people. Dusk had fallen and the lights were on. The Black snorted; he had never seen anything like this. He reared, but Alec brought him down. It was a cool fall night. A breeze blew in through the open door, whipping his mane. His large eyes moved nervously, and he uttered a short, sharp whistle. He shook his head and screamed louder.

Sudden silence fell upon the dock, and all eyes turned toward the Black as he stood in the doorway. Slowly Alec led him down the gangplank. He felt the stallion's black body tremble as the city noises became louder now that the pier was quiet. Halfway down, the Black suddenly went high into the air. Alec brought him down. Three of the crew started up the gangplank to help. The Black saw them and rose again, his legs striking out in front. The men stopped in their tracks. The stallion had broken into a sweat.

Alec knew that he was losing control over him. He took a firmer grip on the rope, holding with two hands. A truck drove onto the pier, its two blazing headlights coming swiftly toward them. The Black screamed and rose once again. Alec was lifted from his feet, still gripping the rope. The stallion flung him to one side; he lost his hold, fell down to the gangplank. High above him he saw the pawing hooves. Cries from the spectators shattered the stillness.

The Black came down, his forelegs landing on each side of Alec's head! He snorted, turned and disappeared inside the hold. Alec lay still, dazed for a moment. Then he felt hands helping him to his feet.

"Are you all right?" one of the men asked.

"Yes, I'm okay," answered Alec. "Just a little shaken."

"You should be after that! He's a wild one!"

A policeman came running up, his gun in one hand. Fear for the Black crept into Alec's heart. He looked at the officer.

"Don't shoot him!" he said.

"I'm not going to," answered the policeman, "unless he endangers any lives."

Alec's strength slowly returned.

"I'll get him," he said.

"I'll go along with you," said the officer. The other men backed down off the gangplank.

"Perhaps I can do this better alone, sir," said Alec.

"Perhaps—but I'll go along just in case——"

Alec entered the hold first. He saw the horse standing

beside his stall. His frightened eyes turned toward the boy.

"What's the matter, fella?" Alec said. "Is New York too much for you?" Cautiously he moved forward and placed his hand on the stallion's neck. The Black moved nervously. "Sure, it's new to you, but it really isn't so bad after you get used to it."

The stallion shoved his nose against Alec's chest. Alec put his hand in his pocket, drew out some sugar and gave it to him. He waited while the wild look gradually left the Black's eyes.

Then he took hold of the halter and led the Black toward the door. The policeman moved to one side. The stallion reared again when he again saw the lights and the crowd. Alec quickly turned him and went back to the stall.

The officer spoke up, "Take off your sweater, kid, and blindfold him."

"Good idea." Quickly he drew off his sweater. He led the stallion to a box, and stepped on it so as to reach his eyes. He folded the sweater and placed it across them, tying it in the back. The stallion jerked his head and tried to toss it off. He half-reared. Alec's assuring hand and voice calmed him down.

Once again he led him toward the door. When they appeared in the doorway, the crowd shouted. Carefully Alec led the stallion down the plank. He saw the stallion's ears prick forward and then go flat back against his head. His breathing became heavier. He shook his head and half-reared again. Alec glanced below; it seemed that thousands of upturned faces were watching them.

Halfway down, the Black again reared into the air. Once again Alec felt himself start to leave the gangplank.

He let the rope slide through his hands. The stallion went high and then descended. Alec dodged the front hoofs. White-faced, he led the Black down. A few more feet and they were on the dock. The crowd shoved aside quickly to get out of the stallion's path.

The Black made a beautiful sight. He moved lightly on his feet; he tossed his head trying to rid himself of the blindfold; his mane waved in the wind. Alec's white sweater across his eyes made a sharp contrast against his coal-black body. "He's getting used to the noises," thought Alec, but he never relaxed his hold on the stallion.

Suddenly he heard his father's voice. "Alec, Alec— here we are!" He turned, saw his mother and father standing on the edge of the crowd—Dad just as tall and thin as ever, Mother just as short and plump. Their faces were as white as the sweater across the Black's eyes. Alec moved toward them, then he remembered the stallion. He saw his mother grip his father's arm. He stopped a short distance away from them.

"Hello, Mother and Dad!" was all he said, though his heart was full. He could see his mother had been crying. Grasping the end of the rope so as to keep hold of the Black, Alec ran up to her, threw his arms around both of them.

"It's good to see you, Alec," his father said after a few minutes.

"It's good to be home," answered Alec. His mother smiled.

The Black moved restlessly beside him. Alec looked at him, then at his parents. "He's mine," he said proudly.

"I was afraid of that," said his father. His mother was too astonished to say anything. He saw his father's eyes going over the stallion. He had done a lot of riding in his day and it was from him that Alec, even as a small child, had learned to love horses. He said nothing, but Alec could tell that he was admiring the Black.

"I'll tell you the whole story later. I owe my life to him."

His mother seemed to have regained control of herself. "But he's so dangerous, son—he threw you down—" But she stopped, puzzled, as she met the calm, self-reliant look in the eyes of the boy who was holding the horse. This couldn't be her son, the boy who had left her only five months ago!

"What are you going to do with him, now that you've got him?" asked his father.

"I don't know, Dad, but I do know where I can keep him!" The words poured out of his mouth. He knew that he must convince his parents right now, once and for all, that the Black must be his—for keeps. "There's that old barn in the old Halleran place up the street where the Daileys are living now. I'm sure they'd let me keep him there for almost nothing, and he'd have a whole acre of ground to graze in! I'll work, Dad, after school, to make money to pay for his feed. Let me keep him, won't you?"

"We'll see, son," said his father quietly. He smiled reassuringly at Alec's mother. "We'll take him home and see how it works out. Only remember, Alec, he's your responsibility—yours to take care of and yours to feed. You've got a big job on your hands. I'll see to it that he gets to Flushing, but from then on it's up to you!"

A young man made his way cautiously around the Black and walked up to them. He carried a camera in one hand, with the other he removed his hat, disclosing hair as black as the stallion's body. "Pardon me," he said to

Alec, "I'm Joe Russo of the *Daily Telegram.* I'd like to take a few pictures and get your story. I understand you're the only survivor of the *Drake* that went down off the coast of Portugal."

Alec pointed to the Black. "He was there, too," he said.

"Say, this *is* a story!" Joe Russo exclaimed. "You mean that horse was on the boat, too?"

"Yes," Alec answered. "He certainly was."

"What happened when the boat sank?" Joe asked, genuinely interested. He wrote hastily with his pencil.

"It's too long to tell you now," Alec replied. "Besides there is so much to be done around here. . . ." He turned to the Black, whose eyes were turning nervously from side to side.

"Let me help you with him," Joe said with all the persistence of a young reporter. "You're going to need a van to get him home, and I think I know where I can get one. Then later on you can give me the whole story!"

"Okay," Alec said, grateful for any assistance with the immediate problem of getting the Black home.

Napoleon

8

An hour later Alec led the Black into a covered truck that Joe Russo had secured to carry him home. His mother had gone ahead, driving the family car. "You won't get me to ride with that horse!" she had said. His father sat in front with Joe Russo and the driver. Alec, afraid to leave the Black alone, stood in the rear with him. The stallion snorted as the truck began to move into the street. His eyes were still covered with the sweater.

Taxicabs roared past, their horns blowing loudly. Trucks rattled toward the ship to pick up cargo. Men shouted in the streets. Cart peddlers clamored their wares. Noise, noise, noise—this was the Black's introduction to New York.

Alec's hand was firm on the halter. Out of the small window in back of the driver he could see the buildings blazing with lights. New York seemed strange to him, too—he had forgotten. The stallion moved uneasily, his head jerked in an attempt to throw off the sweater. "Whoa, Boy," said Alec. He patted the smooth, black coat. Down through the city streets they went.

Alec's father kept looking around, as if he couldn't take his eyes off Alec and the stallion. Slowly the truck moved in and out of the traffic. An elevated train roared overhead. The stallion whistled and half-rose, almost hitting the top of the truck. Alec pulled him down.

Gradually the traffic lessened. They moved farther out of the business section and turned toward Flushing. The worst was over now, and the Black was quiet. Alec was free to think of what fun it was going to be to ride him in that big field near the barn—if they would only let him keep him there.

Then the van was going down the main street of Flushing. Alec peered out the window eagerly. It was good to see the familiar stores and buildings again. Two more blocks and they turned down a side street. Another ten minutes, and Alec saw his own house on the right. His father turned and smiled at him through the window. Alec smiled back.

The truck rolled on past and down the street to the old Halleran house. The van turned into the driveway past a large sign that said TOURISTS. It came to a stop in front of the door.

Alec's father came around to the side of the van. "Okay, Alec," he said, "it's up to you now. Better go in and see whether Mrs. Dailey will let you keep him in the barn."

Alec let go the Black's halter. "Take it easy, Boy," he said. Then he jumped off the van, went up the porch steps and rang the doorbell. The Daileys had moved into the old Halleran place shortly before Alec went to India, so he wasn't very well acquainted with Mrs. Dailey, who now came to the door. She was a large, comfortable-looking, heavy-set woman.

"Hello, Mrs. Dailey," Alec said. "Remember me?"

"Why, you're the young lad from up the street, but they told me—" She paused in obvious amazement. "They told me that you had been drowned in a ship-wreck."

"We were rescued," Alex said. "Just got home to-night."

"Your mother and father must be awfully thankful," she said. "You must have had an awful time!"

"It was pretty bad, Mrs. Dailey—but what I wanted to see you about, Mrs. Dailey, was—well, I brought back a horse with me—we were rescued together."

"A horse!" she exclaimed.

"Yes," said Alec, "and Dad told me I could keep him if I found a place for him to stay. I'd like to put him in one of the stalls in your barn—I'll pay you for it," he added.

"But the barn isn't in very good shape, son," said Mrs. Dailey. She smiled. "And we already have a boarder in the one good stall!"

"A boarder?"

"Yes, Tony, the huckster, keeps old Napoleon down there now."

"Napoleon? Do you mean the old gray horse he's always had?" Alec asked.

"Yes, that's the one—seems to me he should die any day now, though, then you'll be able to use his stall!"

"But I don't know of any other place I could keep my horse, Mrs. Dailey." Alec was beginning to feel desperate. "Don't you have another stall he could use?"

"Well, I suppose the stall right next to Napoleon could be fixed up, but I haven't the time or the money to have it done. If you want to keep your horse there, you'll have to fix it yourself."

"Sure I will, Mrs. Dailey!" said Alec happily. "Could I keep him there tonight?"

"Oh, all right," she gave in with a smile. "And if you do a good job in the barn, I'll go easy on the rent."

"That's swell of you, Mrs. Dailey. I'll do a good job all right!"

"I'll get my husband to open the gate for you," she said. "Henry!" she called loudly. "He'll be down in a few minutes, I suppose. You can drive to the gate—I'll have him meet you there."

"Thanks again, Mrs. Dailey," said Alec. "Thanks a million times." He turned and leaped down the porch steps.

"She's going to let me keep him here!" he shouted as he jumped on the running board of the van.

"That's good," answered his father.

"You're quite a salesman!" laughed Joe Russo. Alec saw that he was making notes on his pad.

"Wait until she sees what's going to stay in her barn!" said Alec's father gravely.

They drove past a high iron fence until they reached the gate. There they stopped and waited for Henry. Finally he showed up—a short, chunky man with large shoulders. He came toward them walking in jerky, bowlegged strides. His white shirt tails flapped in the night wind. He wiped a large hand across his mouth. "Right with you," he yelled. He shoved a key inside the lock and then pushed back the heavy gate; the hinges creaked as it swung open. "Come on," he said.

The van rolled through and went up the gravel road to the barn. The headlights shone on the large door. Henry came up behind them. "I'll open the door," he said, "and you can bring him right in."

Alec let down the side door of the van so that he could get the stallion out. He grasped the halter. "It's your new home, Boy!" he said. Slowly he led the stallion down to the ground. The Black tossed his head and kicked up his heels.

"Look at him!" said Alec. "He feels swell already!" He saw the men gazing admiringly at the stallion.

Henry leaned on the barn door; his eyes moved slowly over the Black. "The Missus told me you had a horse— but I never expected one like this!" He shook his head. "Good head, wide chest, strong legs," he muttered, almost to himself.

Alec led the Black into the barn. In the box stall nearest the door was Napoleon, his old gray head hanging out over the stall door. He whinnied when he saw the Black and drew his head back into the stall.

"Shall I put him next to Napoleon there, Mr. Dailey?" Alec asked. "Do you think it'll be safe? He gets pretty nervous sometimes."

"Sure, put him there. Old Napoleon will be more of a help to him than anything—steady him down." Henry went over to a corner of the barn and picked up a bale of straw which he carried back into the stall and spread around. "We'll borrow some of Tony's straw for bedding. He won't mind. Now you can put him in, son," he said. "There are a few things that need to be fixed, but I guess it'll hold him—you can do a better job tomorrow."

"Thanks," Alec said.

"What are you going to feed him tonight, Alec? Did you think of that?" his father asked.

"Gee, that's right!" said Alec. "I *had* forgotten!" He turned to Henry. "Where do you think I could get some feed, Mr. Dailey?"

"Well, Tony gets his down at the feed store on the corner of Parsons and Northern, but I imagine they're closed now. But you can use some of Tony's and pay him back when you get your own."

"Great," answered Alec. He led the Black into the stall next to Napoleon's. It was a little run-down, but it was roomy, and Alec could tell that the stallion liked it. He stood very patiently while Alec removed his halter and rubbed him down. Then Henry handed Alec a pail of feed and Alec dumped it into the Black's box.

Old Napoleon stuck his head curiously over the board between the stalls. The Black saw him, strode over and sniffed suspiciously. Napoleon didn't move. Alec was afraid they might fight. Then the Black put his head over into Napoleon's stall and whinnied. Napoleon whinnied back.

Henry laughed. "See, what'd I tell you? They're friends already."

Alec left the stall, feeling more easy about the Black than at any time since they had begun the long journey home. "I'm glad he liked Napoleon," he said. "Perhaps I can leave him now. He has to learn to be alone sometime."

"He looks as though he'll be all right," said his father. "In fact, he seems to like it here. He isn't so wild, after all!"

"He's all right, Dad, when he gets used to things. It's

just when something new upsets him that he gets out of control."

"Well, son, let's go home and see your mother. She's probably worrying herself to death."

Joe Russo spoke up. "I hate to make a nuisance of myself, Mr. Ramsay, but I'd like to go along and get your son's story. It has all the earmarks of a good yarn and I certainly could use one!"

Alec's father smiled. "Sure, it's all right. Glad to have you. This is a day of celebration for us, you know!"

Henry led the way out of the barn. Alec heard the Black's soft whistle as the light went out. Then there was silence. Henry shut the barn door.

A slight chill had crept into the air. The van had already gone. They walked slowly down the gravel road toward the gate. Henry handed Alec the key to the lock. "You can have this, son," he said. "I've another up to the house, and you'll probably be coming around here a lot now."

"Thanks, Mr. Dailey," replied Alec. "I certainly will."

"That's all right—and you don't have to call me Mr. Dailey—just call me Henry like everyone does around here. Anything else seems kind of funny!"

"Right, Henry."

Henry left them at the gate. They crossed the street and walked up toward the house. Alec saw a light on the front porch and his legs traveled faster.

"Take it easy," said his father. "I'm not as young as I used to be, you know!"

"I can't even keep up with that pace myself," laughed Joe, "and I'm still pretty young."

"I'll meet you there," said Alec, and he broke into a run.

He reached the house and took the porch steps two at a time. He flung himself at the door. It was unlocked; he ran into the hallway and glanced into the living room; it was empty. He put a hand on the banister and started up the stairs. Then he heard his mother's voice from the kitchen. "Alexander, is that you?"

"Yes, Mom, it's really me," he yelled. He ran into the kitchen and flung his arms around his mother. "Boy, it's good to be home!" he said.

He looked up at his mother and saw that her eyes were moist. "What's the matter, Mom? What are you crying for?"

Mrs. Ramsay smiled through her tears. "Nothing's the matter. I'm just glad you're home, that's all."

Alec put his lean brown arm through his mother's soft plump one, and together they went into the living room as his father and Joe Russo came in from outdoors.

The reporter looked around the room with its soft shaded lights and its comfortable-looking furniture, then at Alec and his father and mother. "Guess you couldn't blame him for wanting to get back to this," Joe said.

"You bet!" Alec agreed.

His mother sat down on the couch and Alec sat beside her, his arm still in hers. His father was filling his pipe in his favorite chair in the corner. "All right, son," he said. "Tell us all about it."

"Well," Alec began, "it was a few days after I left Uncle Ralph at Bombay that we stopped at a small Arabian port on the Red Sea——"

The clock on top of the radio ticked off the minutes as

Alec told his story. Once more he was on the *Drake* and seeing the Black for the first time. He forgot that his mother, his father and Joe Russo were listening to him. He was in the storm, hearing the roar of the gale and the smashing of the waves against the boat. He heard the loud crack of lightning as it struck the ship. Then the Black was dragging him through the water—hours and hours they battled the waves in the darkness. He roamed the island, fighting against starvation. He discovered the carragheen that had saved them both. He rode the stallion for the first time—that wild, never-to-be-forgotten ride! Then the fire, that awful fire, which turned out to be a blessing in disguise. The joy that was his when he saw the sailors dragging their boat up the beach. Rio de Janeiro—home. . . .

He finished, and there was silence. His mother's hand was gripping his. The clock ticked loudly. It seemed to say, "You're home . . . you're home . . ."

His father's pipe had gone out. "I don't know what to say, son"—he broke the silence—"except that God must have been with you—and with us." He turned to Mrs. Ramsay. "We're pretty thankful, aren't we, Mother?"

Alec felt the pressure of her hand. "Yes," she answered, "we have much to be thankful for."

"I can understand now how you love that horse," Joe Russo said.

"Yes, Alec," said his father, "I can promise you now he'll always have a place here with us."

"If it wasn't for him—that wild, untamed animal——" his mother said.

Joe Russo stood up. "I want to thank you for letting me stay," he said. "If there is anything I can ever do——"

Mr. Ramsay rose from his chair. "That's all right. Glad to have helped you," he said. "Good night." He held out his hand.

"Good night, sir." He smiled at Alec and his mother. "Take good care of that horse," he said to the boy.

"You bet I will," answered Alec. "And thanks for all you've done."

Not long after Joe left, Alec said good night to his parents and went to bed. The excitement of being home and sleeping in his own bed again made him restless. He lay awake for an hour, then he fell into a sound sleep.

Suddenly a shrill whistle awakened him. He opened his eyes sleepily. Had he been dreaming or had he actually heard the Black scream? The night was still. A minute passed. Then he heard the whistle again—it was the Black.

Alec jumped out of bed. The clock on his dresser told him it was only a little after twelve! He was wide awake as he pulled on his robe and quickly ran down the stairs and out the door. He heard the Black scream again as he entered the gate. Lights flashed on in Henry's house— then in the houses near by. The Black was waking everyone up! Alec sprinted toward the barn. He reached the door. The light was on!

The Black screamed when he saw him. His head reached far out over the stall.

"Dio mio!" a voice was moaning from inside Napoleon's stall. Alec couldn't see anybody—only old Napoleon, who stood trembling on the far side of his stall. His frightened eyes turned beseechingly toward Alec. *"Dio mio!"* came the voice again.

"Hello," yelled Alec. "Who's there?"

The Black pawed nervously at the floor of his stall. Then Alec saw a hand move over the top of Napoleon's door and cautiously push it open. Suddenly, like a charging fullback, a man plunged through the stall door.

He swept past and was outside before Alec could catch a glimpse of him. The Black whistled again. "Hey, Black," yelled Alec, "take it easy!" Then he ran toward the door and looked out into the night. Alec saw a man standing beside Henry, who had just arrived on the scene. It was Tony, the huckster, owner of Napoleon! Poor Tony, he'd probably been frightened to death at sight of the Black in the stall next to Napoleon!

"Hello, Tony," Alec called as he made his way toward him. Some of the neighbors, their robes pulled hastily about them, were coming up the driveway. Then the sound of a police siren reached Alec's ears. "Gosh," he said as a police car turned into the driveway. "Tony, you're all right, aren't you?" he asked.

"Sure, he's all right," answered Henry, grinning. "The Black just surprised him."

Tony only nodded. He was still too scared to speak. A small crowd gathered around them. "What's the matter here?" asked the policeman as he got out of his car.

"Nothing serious, officer," Henry spoke up. "I own this barn and took in another horse tonight, unknown to Tony here. They both sorta surprised each other—that's about all there is to it."

"That right?" the officer asked Tony.

Tony found his voice. *"Si,"* he said, "that's-a right. I ver' busy make-a better the harness sore on my Nappy when I look-a up and see heem. He sure make-a me the surprise all right."

The crowd laughed at Tony's comments. "Well," said the policeman, "guess everything's all right around here then. Who owns the horse?"

"I do, sir," Alec answered.

"You're rather young to own a horse that does such a big job of scaring people." The officer smiled.

"I just brought him to New York yesterday," Alec replied. "He's still pretty nervous, but he'll get over it."

"He sounds like quite a horse. Would you mind letting me take a look at him?" the policeman asked.

"Be glad to," Alec said.

The small crowd moved forward, pushing Tony in front of them. Alec stopped at the door of the barn. "Most of you will have to watch from here," he said. "Too many people will get him excited again."

The Black neighed softly as Henry, Alec, Tony and the policeman approached the stall. Napoleon stuck his head over the stall door and neighed at sight of Tony, who hung back. The Black still pawed at the floor of his stall. Alec rubbed his nose.

"He's a beauty," the policeman said. "I've always had a weakness for horses ever since I spent two years on the mounted force. Don't know as I've ever seen one like this, though." He paused, then after watching the Black a few minutes, he continued, "Yep, looks like everything's okay around here—and I have to get back to the station. So long." He left, taking the crowd with him.

Tony stayed in the barn with Alec and Henry. Gingerly he moved toward Napoleon, keeping one watchful eye on the Black. The stallion pushed his head forward. He neighed. "He likes you and Napoleon," Alec said.

Tony reached a hand to the Black's muzzle, then

jerked it away quickly as the stallion shook his head. Alec and Henry laughed. *"Si,"* said Tony, "I like-a heem too, after a while!"

A short time later, Alec once again climbed the stairs to his bedroom. Luckily his parents were both sound sleepers—it was better that they didn't know of the commotion the Black had made.

Alec climbed wearily back into bed. He was really tired now. He glanced at the clock—two-fifteen—and he wanted to be over to the barn early the next morning! His head fell back on the pillow. He was soon fast asleep.

Escape

9

The next morning when Alec opened his eyes, he saw the familiar high school banners hanging on the walls. It was good to be in his own room again. Then right away he wondered how the Black was after his rumpus of last night! Alec turned on his side and looked out the window. The sun was rising. It must be around six o'clock.

Not much sleep—but then he was accustomed to that after the last few months. The leaves on the trees were turning a bright autumn red. He was glad his father had told him he wouldn't have to go to school today. "One more day won't hurt," he had said, "and it'll give you a chance to accustom yourself again." He knew what his father had really meant was that it would give him a chance to accustom the Black to his new surroundings!

Alec jumped out of bed and ran to the bathroom. He took a cold shower, dressed and tiptoed down the stairs. He opened the door and went out into the crisp morning air. It was quiet as only early morning can be. The grass was wet with a heavy dew. He walked down the street, softly whistling to himself. A safe distance away from the house he began to sing.

He found the gate ajar. Someone must be there already—perhaps Tony! He ran up the road toward the barn, and heard a deep bass voice coming from inside. *"San—ta Lu—ci—a, Santa Lu—cia!"* Sure, that couldn't be anyone else but Tony! The barn door was open. Alec saw the little Italian sitting on a chair, his eyes fastened on the two stalls from which were coming deep munching sounds.

"Hello, Tony!"

Tony turned, his dark, wrinkled face creasing into a broad smile. "Hello," he said. "You see, I'm not afraid of heem any more!"

"Yes," Alec laughed, "I can see that. You'll get along swell with him as time goes on!"

"Ah, he's one great fella—make-a me think when Napoleon was-a young! So frisky, so full of pep, and when he saw me feed Napoleon, he let me feed heem too!"

"That's pretty good, Tony. Usually he won't let anyone get near him but me."

"Look at them," Tony said.

Napoleon had shoved his nose through the bars and was trying to get at the Black's feed box. The stallion playfully nipped him. Napoleon withdrew his head and looked over the stall door.

"Time to go to work, young fella," laughed Tony. He let him out of the stall, and rubbed his hand over the gray, ragged coat. "Tomorrow I give heem a good bath so he'll be white as snow!" he said.

Alec watched Tony harness Napoleon. He saw him tenderly arrange a thick pad over the cut on Napoleon's shoulder. He noticed that the Black was also an interested spectator.

"Give me a hand, will you, Alec? We're kinda late this morning," Tony said.

Alec helped to harness old Napoleon to the little huckster's wagon. It seemed child's play to handle the gentle old gray horse after the spirited stallion.

They heard the Black scream inside. Alec ran into the barn. "What's the matter, Black?" he said.

The long black neck was stretched questioningly into the next stall. He missed Napoleon.

"Napoleon has to go to work, Boy, but he'll be back tonight." Alec opened the door and took the Black by the halter. He grabbed the lead rope from a nail outside the stall and fastened it to the halter. Then he led the Black out.

Tony was climbing into the seat of the wagon. "Well, Alec, we gotta go," he said. "See you tonight. Come on, Napoleon."

Napoleon raised his head and neighed as he saw the Black. He refused to move. Tony shook the reins. "Come on, now, Nappy. We gotta go!" he repeated. Napoleon shook his head, looked at the Black, then resignedly started off.

The Black pulled at the rope. He wanted to follow. Alec held him back. He reared high into the air; his ears pitched forward and he snorted angrily.

Alec smiled. "Hate to see your roommate leave, don't you?"

They watched Tony and Napoleon go slowly down the

gravel road to the gate. Napoleon broke into a slow trot down the street.

When they were out of sight, the Black moved in a circle around Alec.

"Feeling pretty good, aren't you, Boy?" Alec let the rope out to give the Black more room. He led him toward the open field, encircled by a stone wall. "You're going to like this to graze in," he said. "Just look at all that grass!"

The Black cropped the green grass hungrily. When he seemed to have had enough, Alec ran down the field with him. "Not too fast now, Black!" Alec called as the stallion cantered ahead of him. Halfway down the field he found himself tiring and pulled the Black to a halt.

"How about giving me a ride now, Black?" he asked. He looked for a place to mount him. He drew the stallion alongside the stone wall, climbed up on it and slid onto the Black, grasping the halter with both hands.

He hadn't had a chance to ride him since the island. The Black stood still a moment, then broke into a trot. Alec was able to guide him fairly well with the halter and he found that the stallion still remembered his lessons on the island.

Down the field they went, the wind whipping in Alec's face, the early morning stillness echoing with the stallion's hoofbeats. His long powerful strides made the field seem much too small. Alec turned him around the edge and started him back up the field. They went faster and faster. Alec dug his knees into the stallion's sides and his own body moved rhythmically with the Black's. They swept past the barn and Alec turned him back down the field again. Around and around the field they went.

After a while Alec managed to slow him down a bit. The Black continued around the field at a gallop. Then he slackened into a trot. Alec had never been happier. Home at last—and with a horse like this! All his very own! He buried his head in the Black's mane and wiped his hand across his eyes, drying the tears the wind had brought to them.

They approached the barn. Alec saw Henry Dailey leaning against the door watching them. He rode up to him and dismounted, catching hold of the stallion's halter. "Morning, Henry," he said. He felt the Black's coat. "Not even wet. . . . What a horse, Henry! We've been going around that field like the wind! Did you see us?"

Henry didn't move from the door but Alec saw his small gray eyes going over the Black inch by inch. "Sure, I saw you," he said. "Son, I've seen a lot of horses in my day and rode my share of 'em, but I never saw one give any better exhibition than that!"

Alec beamed with pride. "He is swell, Henry, isn't he? I still can't believe he's mine!" The stallion's long neck reached down to the ground and he buried his nose in the green grass.

"Let him loose, Alec. See how he likes it," said Henry.

"Do you think it's safe?"

"He's all right now. You gave him a good run. Besides he has to get used to being left alone, anyway."

"Guess you're right, Henry." Alec unsnapped the lead rope from the halter. The stallion raised his head and his nostrils quivered. Suddenly he wheeled and trotted swiftly down the field.

Alec and Henry watched him. "It's the first freedom

he's had in a long time," said Alec.

"And he's sure enjoying it." Henry looked after the Black admiringly.

The stallion stopped and turned his great head toward them. He whistled softly.

"Boy, I'd love to see him on a track!" Henry said thoughtfully.

"You mean race, Henry?" Alec asked.

"Yep."

Alec turned to the Black, who was now loping down the field again in an easy, graceful canter, his head turning from side to side. "It'd take a long time before he'd be safe on any track though, Henry."

"Well, we have plenty of time, haven't we, Alec?"

"We?" Alec stared at the small husky man beside him. "You mean, Henry, that you and I could do it?"

Henry hadn't moved—his eyes still followed the Black around the field. "Sure, we can," he said quietly, and then his voice lowered so that Alec could hardly hear him. "Never liked this business of retiring, anyway," he said. "Not too old—still have plenty of good years left in me! This life's all right for the Missus—she's got enough to do to keep her busy, but I need action. And here I have it shoved right into my lap!" His voice grew louder. "Alec," he continued, "I know we can make a champion out of the Black." His face was wrinkled with excitement, his eyelids narrowed until they were only slits in his lined face.

"You really mean it, Henry? But how——"

The old man interrupted him and he moved for the first time. "Sure, I'm confident, Alec, and I know my horses." He took the boy by the arm. "Come with me and I'll show you something."

Henry led him to the far end of the barn. He knelt down beside an old trunk. He took a key from his pocket, inserted it into the lock and opened it. The trunk was crammed to the top with trophies and silver cups. Henry dug down and pulled out a large scrapbook. "The Missus always kept this for me, even before we were married."

He turned the faded yellowish pages that were filled with newspaper clippings. Headline after headline caught Alec's eye as he knelt beside Henry: DAILEY RIDES CHANG TO VICTORY IN SCOTT MEMORIAL—DAILEY BRINGS WARRIOR HOME FIRST IN $50,000 FUTURITY—TURFDOM ACCLAIMS DAILEY AS GREATEST RIDER OF ALL TIME—Henry stopped turning the pages, his eyes gazing steadily at a photograph in front of him. "This, son," he said, "is where I got the greatest thrill of my life—riding Chang home first in the Kentucky Derby. Wouldn't think that little guy there was me, would you?"

Alec looked closer. He saw a small boy, with a wide grin on his face, astride a large, powerful-looking red horse. Around the horse's neck hung the winner's horseshoe of roses. Alec noticed the large, strong hands holding the reins and the stocky, broad shoulders. "Yes," he said, "I can tell that's you."

Henry smiled and reached down into the trunk again. He took out what looked to Alec like old dried-out leaves. Then he saw that they were in the shape of a horseshoe. He looked again at the photograph.

"Yes," Henry said, "it's the same one they placed around Chang's neck that day. Not much left of 'em, but they still hold plenty of memories!"

Henry put the dried flowers back into the trunk. "When I finally got too old and too heavy to ride horses any more, I trained them instead," he continued. "I married the Missus and we were both pretty happy. We had two children—both girls; now they're married. Somehow, I've always missed not having a boy—someone like you, son, who loved horses, and who would sort of follow in my footsteps, because there isn't anything so exciting in the world as lining up there at the post with a four-legged piece of dynamite underneath you!

"Well, to go on, I was pretty successful as a trainer, made good money. And then came the day when the Missus thought it was time for us to retire and get away from the track. Can't say as I blame her, it's the only life she ever knew after she married me, and I guess it wasn't in her blood like it was in mine. We did a lot of movin' around for a good many years, then we bought this place, and here we are. It's been two years since I saw my last race—two years. I don't think I can stand it much longer."

Henry paused again. "You see, Alec," he said, "I'm telling you this to show you that if there is only one thing that I do know anything about it's whether a horse is any good or not—and let me tell you we can make the Black the greatest racer that ever set a hoof on any track!"

Henry closed the book with a sharp crack and placed it back inside the trunk. He rose to his feet and put his hand on the boy's shoulder. "What do you say, son—are you game?"

Alec looked at the old man and then toward the open door where he could see the Black in the distance. "It would be great, Henry!" he said, "and I know he would give any horse in the world a real race—if we can just keep him from fighting."

"It'll be a tough job, Alec, but it's going to be worth it to see him come pounding down the homestretch!"

"Where can we train him, Henry?"

"We can't do much until spring, Alec—just let him get used to it around here. You can ride him around the field and I'll teach you all the tricks I know. We won't be able to do much else with him with winter coming on. I don't think we'll even bother with a bridle and saddle yet—we'll wait until early spring for that, too. By that time we shouldn't have much trouble putting them on him. Then I think I can find a way to get him over to Belmont for some workouts on the track—that's when the real training begins!"

"Sounds swell, Henry! Do you think I'll be able to ride him in the races?"

Henry smiled. "Unless I'm very much mistaken, that horse isn't going to let anyone else ride him."

As they walked toward the door, the loud drone of an airplane filled the air. "That fellow's awfully close to the ground!" said Alec. "His motor seems to be missing, too!"

They ran outside and saw a plane flying low over the barn; its motor stuttered and then caught again, shattering the early morning stillness with a deafening roar. "He's got it!" said Henry.

But Alec wasn't watching the plane now; he had heard something above the plane's roar. The sharp, piercing whistle of the Black! Alec saw the stallion rise on his hind legs and wheel in the air, running at breakneck speed down the field.

"Look, Henry!" Alec shouted. "The Black!" The stallion was nearing the end of the field, his pace never slackening, his long, black mane whipping behind him like waves of smoke.

"Lord!" said Henry. "The plane scared him! He'll kill himself on those rocks!"

"He's not going to stop, Henry!" Then they saw the Black gather himself, and, like a taut, powerful spring just released, sail through the air and over the fence.

"Seven feet if it's an inch!" exclaimed Henry. "Come on, we've got to get him!" Together they rushed down the field. They saw the Black in the distance—then he was out of sight! Suddenly Henry stopped. "I'll go back and get the car, Alec. You keep after him!" he said.

"All right," Alec shouted over his shoulder. "He's headed for the park!" Quickly he climbed the fence, and ran as fast as he could in the direction the stallion had taken. Soon Henry caught up to him in the car. "Climb in, son," he said. The Black was nowhere to be seen.

The Search

10

For half an hour Alec and Henry frantically looked for the Black. Up and down the streets they sped in Henry's car.

"Lucky it's so early in the morning, Alec—not so many people around," Henry said.

"What time is it?" Alec asked, never taking his eyes off the road in front of him.

Henry pulled his large silver watch out of his vest pocket. "Seven o'clock," he grunted.

"We've just got to find him, Henry—before it's too late!" the boy declared.

"What do you mean—too late?" Henry asked.

"I'm afraid of some cops shooting him. Gosh! That would be terrible!"

Henry nodded and pushed his foot harder on the accelerator. The car jumped ahead.

"Turn down this street, Henry—the park's just ahead; maybe he's there."

Alec saw two men on a street corner. "Pull over there, Henry. We'll ask them if they've seen him. They seem to be pretty excited over something!"

Alec leaned out of the car. "Say, Mister," he yelled, "did you see a horse run down here?"

"Sure did," one of them answered. "He shot past here like a streak of lightning ten minutes ago! Where the devil did he come from?"

"Thanks," said Alec without answering the man's question. The car lurched ahead as Henry stepped on the gas.

"We're on the right track, anyway, Alec," Henry said grimly. A few minutes later they entered the park. Henry slowed down. "You look over there, kid—I'll take care of this side."

"It's an awfully big park," Alec said, discouraged.

"All the better," grinned Henry. "Not much chance of him hurting anyone then!"

The car rolled through tree-lined roads. Henry and Alec both leaned out the sides of the car. After a few miles they approached the rolling green fairways of the golf course.

"He might have gone out there, Henry," Alec said. "Plenty of hills, just what he'd be looking for."

"Let's park the car here and take a look, Alec," Henry said as he brought the car to a stop.

Alec had to trot to keep up with Henry's short but energetic strides across the fairway. The air was cool and crisp, but starting to warm up from the bright sun that was climbing higher and higher in the cloudless blue sky.

Their shoes made deep squishing sounds in the early morning dew.

"Going to be a hot day," muttered Henry, never slowing his pace. Alec jogged beside him. "Hope we can find him before the early morning golfers start coming out," he said.

When they reached the middle of the fairway, Henry stopped. "You'd better go in the direction of that wood over there," he said. "I'll go down this fairway a piece toward that hill. If either of us finds him, give a yell."

"Okay, Henry," Alec said. He started off in the direction of the wood. His feet were soaked. He stopped and started to remove his shoes, then thinking better of it, straightened up and continued at a fast pace. He went down into a large gully. At the bottom he turned and followed the gully as it wove in and out across the fairway. Soon he entered the wood. He climbed to the top of the gully and looked about. Henry was out of sight. The dew on the green grass glistened in the distance. The air was quiet and cooler in the shade of the big trees. Alec knew that on the other side of the wood was another fairway. He hastened toward it, following the path which he had traveled many times as a caddy during the summer months.

He reached the other side and looked across the stretch of green carpet spread before him. The Black was nowhere to be seen. Alec whistled—but there was no answer. He started across the fairway. "Still have a lot of ground to cover," he thought. "He's liable to be any place."

For what seemed hours, Alec trudged up and down the hills of the course looking for the Black. The sun was higher now and hotter. He became more and more desperate as he saw no sign of the stallion. He removed his white sweater and flung it over his arm. He reached the top of a high hill and looked below him. In the distance he could see some men playing golf.

"Henry might have found him," he thought hopefully. He had covered more than half the course and the Black surely wasn't around here. Alec whistled again. If the Black was within hearing distance, he surely would recognize his whistle. But there was no answering call.

Perhaps the stallion hadn't entered the park at all. Perhaps he was still somewhere in the streets. But Alec felt the stallion was too intelligent for that. His natural instinct would lead him to the open spaces here in the park. He *must* be around somewhere! Alec began to climb back down the hill toward the fairway. He had covered his territory thoroughly. Then he stopped. He hadn't been to the Hole where he and the fellows always went for a swim after their day of caddying. It was off the course, but there was a chance the stallion's instinct had led him toward the water.

He had to look there—he mustn't let even a slim chance slip by. Alec turned in his tracks and went alongside the hill. His legs ached, and his wet feet weren't helping matters any. He walked about a mile before he came to another wood. He followed a well-hidden path down into a hollow and then up again. It was at least nice and cool in here. The Hole was just ahead now. Alec quickened his steps. He reached the top of the hill and looked down. The water glistened below him. The pool wasn't large and if the Black was there, he surely would see him. But there wasn't any sign of him.

The wood was quiet except for the staccato-like tapping

of a hard-working woodpecker in a nearby tree. Hope faded within Alec—he had played his last hunch. It was the natural place for the Black to be—the only pool of water for miles around. He took one final look. Even the shadows on the side of the pool wouldn't have been able to conceal the stallion. He just wasn't there.

Back along the path he climbed wearily. What had happened to his horse? He saw the Black lying dead in the street, killed by a car or by a policeman's bullets. It just couldn't be—it couldn't end that way! Probably Henry had found him already.

A sharp, cracking noise broke the stillness. He whirled. It came from the direction of the pool. He hurried back and looked down. On the other side, something was making its way through the thick underbrush and coming in the direction of the water! Alec stood still, scarcely daring to hope! There wasn't any path over there. Whatever it was, was making its own way through the bushes. The noise became louder and louder. Then suddenly a huge black head appeared. It was the Black! Alec saw him reach his long neck down and bury his nose into the cool water.

Relief paralyzed him for a moment. Then he whistled softly. The Black raised his head, water dripping from his mouth. He looked up. Alec whistled again and ran down the slope toward the pool. The stallion saw him. He shook his head and whistled. Alec slowed down to a walk. Cautiously he covered the distance around the pool and approached the Black.

"What's the matter, fella—scared?" he asked.

The stallion shook his head and moved toward him. His black coat was dirty and his long mane covered with burrs. Alec patted the dripping muzzle. "Had a tough time, didn't you, Boy!" He ran his hand down the stallion's neck, wiping the dirt off. "It's sure good to see you!" he said.

The stallion again pushed his nose into the cool water and drank deep. When he had finished, Alec grasped the halter that was still around his head. "Come on, Boy, let's get going home."

The Black refused to move. Alec spoke softly to him and rubbed a hand across his neck, but the stallion stood firm. Alec pulled on the halter again. The Black's eyes swept around, then rested on the boy. He shook his head and slowly moved after him.

Alec led him up the path through the wood. When they reached the fairway, he stopped and looked at the horse. "Wouldn't give a guy a lift, would you, Mister?" he asked. The Black moved swiftly to one side, his eyes turned toward the open fairway. "I'm really pretty tired, Black—you gave me quite a chase, you know." He led the Black over to a tree stump, stepped on it and threw himself onto the stallion's back.

"Come on, Boy," he said, "let's go."

The Black walked fast out onto the fairway, and then broke into a trot. Alec turned him toward the spot where he had left Henry. "Better get off this course in a hurry," he thought, "or they'll have the riot squad after us for tearing up the ground!"

After riding for about five minutes, Alec saw Henry in the distance walking toward them. "Had just about given up," Henry said when Alec rode up. "I almost did, too," Alec said. "Found him away over by the Hole."

"Looks as though he's been rolling around in the dirt."

"He's had a time for himself, all right," Alec answered. "Look at the burrs on him—must have gone through a lot of underbrush."

"We can get those off." Henry glanced at his watch. "But right now we'd better be getting back—almost nine o'clock."

For the first time Alec realized that he had had no breakfast and that his parents didn't even know where he was. "Mother'll be wondering what's happened to me," Alec said. Late for his first breakfast home!

"And the Missus isn't going to be welcoming me with eager arms, either," Henry said gravely. "Promised her I'd go down to the market this morning, but it's too late now."

Alec jumped off the Black and walked beside Henry, holding the Black by his halter. Soon they reached the car. "Better go by way of Colden Street," Henry said, "and miss the traffic. Guess you'll have to lead him— that's the only way."

"You drive ahead slowly, Henry, just in case I need you," Alec said.

The car rolled out of the park and Alec and the Black followed it. Twenty minutes later, after no mishaps, they neared the stable. The stallion's ears pricked forward when he saw the barn. "I'm going to have to build that fence higher, Henry," Alec yelled.

"'Fraid so," answered Henry, "or we'll be spending half our time chasing this fellow around!"

Henry drove up to the barn, and Alec followed with the Black. "I'll put him in his stall for the rest of the day, Henry," he said.

"Good idea," replied Henry. "He's sure had enough exercise for one day, and so have I."

"Me, too," answered Alec. "I'll put him away and then go home and eat. I'll come back later and clean him up."

"Okay, son. I'll probably be seeing you—that is," he laughed, "if I can get out!" He turned and walked toward the house.

Alec put the Black in his stall and ran a brush over his body. He put some hay in the stallion's feed box. "There, that'll hold you until I get back," he said. "Be a good fellow now and take it easy, won't you?"

The stallion pawed his foreleg into the straw and shook his head. "You'd better behave," said Alec, laughing. "You've caused enough trouble for one day." He shut the barn door and made his way home.

Alec heard the living-room clock strike nine-thirty as he walked into the house. "That you, Alec?" His mother's voice came anxiously from the kitchen.

"Yes, Mom," he answered, as he walked into the room. "Dad gone to work?" His nose wrinkled as he sniffed the appetizing aroma of griddle cakes and sausages.

"Yes," his mother answered. "He wanted to see you, but he couldn't wait any longer. Where on earth have you been all this time? And just look at you!"

"I've been exercising the Black, Mom," Alec answered. He didn't know whether he should tell his mother about the Black running away. He decided against it—it would only worry her more, and now that the stallion was back, everything was all right.

"You certainly spend a lot of time with that animal," his mother said. "I don't know what you're going to do when you have to go to school."

Alec walked over to the kitchen table and sat down. He

felt the water oozing out of his shoes. "Oh, I'm going to get up early every morning, Mom," he said, "and feed and groom him before I go to school." He fumbled with his shoelaces underneath the table, attempting to get his shoes off without his mother's noticing him.

"When the weather's nice," he continued, "I'm going to leave him outside to graze during the morning. I'll be in the early session at school this term and have classes right through, and get out at twelve-thirty. That'll give me lots of time in the afternoon to be with him." Alec slipped his shoes and socks off and wound his feet around the legs of the chair.

"I don't want you to neglect your studies, Alec," his mother said. "If I see you doing that, I'll have to tell your father, and we'll have to do something about the Black."

"He won't interfere, Mom," Alec answered, as he hungrily applied butter and maple syrup to the griddle cakes his mother placed before him. Life was settling down to normal again—as normal as it could ever be with the Black.

Partners

11

The rest of the day passed quickly for Alec. After breakfast, while his mother was in the living room, he slipped upstairs and put on dry shoes and socks. When he came down, he chatted with his mother, sharing little incidents of his experiences on the island and telling her about Uncle Ralph and the fun they had had together in India. In the afternoon he groomed the Black until the stallion's black body glistened, and his long mane fell smoothly down on his neck.

Henry came into the stable. "Been cleaning the attic," he grunted. He carried a large package wrapped in newspapers under his arm. He placed the bundle down on the floor. "Come here and look what I found," he said to Alec.

He began unwrapping the package, as Alec knelt beside him. The papers, brown with age, cracked and fell apart as he took them off. Inside was a small racing saddle and bridle. Henry gently lifted them out and looked at them. He didn't say anything. A minute passed and then he reached down into the bundle again. Almost caressingly he drew out a blazing green jockey cap and shirt. Alec looked down into the bundle and saw a faded pair of riding pants and black boots.

Henry spoke softly. "Everything's here—even my number." He held the shirt in his hand. Around the sleeve still hung the white number 3. "Seems like only yesterday I wore 'em in the last race I ever rode."

Henry stopped. Alec didn't speak—he could tell from Henry's face that once again he was living that race over.

"We went to the post," the little man said, as if to himself. "It was the largest crowd ever to see the International Cup. They were all for Chang, too—he was the greatest race horse of the day. How they roared when we lined up. The other horses wouldn't stand still. But nothing ever bothered Chang—he let the others do the frisking. He just waited quietly for the barrier to go up.

"I never saw the rest of 'em in that race. Chang leaped ahead at the start, and I gave him his head—we won going away." Henry swept a hand across his eyes. "It wasn't until he had come to a stop that he suddenly trembled, staggered, vainly attempted to keep his feet, then fell to the ground dead. The doctors never knew what actually killed him—finally said that it was a blood clot or something like that. I never knew what to believe. The only thing that mattered was that Chang was gone— but the record he set that day still stands."

Henry stopped and his gaze turned to the Black.

"I never thought I would see a horse that could break that record—until now," he said. The Black's long neck stretched far over his stall door. He shook his head and whinnied.

Carefully Henry put the shirt back into the bundle and rose to his feet. He carried it over to the corner of the barn and placed it inside the trunk. Then he turned around and faced the boy. "There's just one thing that stands in our way of putting the Black in a race, Alec."

"You mean because he's so wild, Henry?"

"No, I don't mean that. By spring we should have him calmed down a bit. But I read in the paper just now of how you got the Black. You didn't tell me this morning."

"I was going to, Henry, but why does that stand in his way?"

"Only that you don't have any record of who his sire and dam were, and Alec, a horse must be registered to run in a race."

Alec felt a sick feeling in his stomach—he hadn't realized how much he had looked forward to seeing the Black race. "You mean, Henry, we have to find that out before we can put the Black on a track?"

"'Fraid so, kid," Henry answered. Alec could see that he was as disappointed as himself. "Isn't there any way you could possibly get that information?" the little man asked.

"I don't see how, Henry. I know the name of the port in Arabia where he got on, but that's all. Everyone on the ship was drowned, so there aren't any records we could possibly get."

Henry thought a minute. Then he said, "I'll drop a line to a friend of mine in the Jockey Club. Maybe he can help us—some way."

"Gee, Henry, I hope so!"

"We have all winter to try and find out," Henry said.

"Maybe they can trace him from the town or somethin'. He looks like too valuable a horse not to be registered in a Stud Book somewhere!" He walked toward the door. "Have to be gettin' back now or the Missus'll be comin' down for me!" He stopped and put a hand in his pocket. He took out a piece of paper. "Wrote down what we need for the Black to eat, Alec," he said. "After you get finished, you can go down to the feed store and get 'em. We can't have the big boy eating all of Napoleon's grain, you know." He paused and his hand went once again inside his pocket. "Seein' that we're goin' to work together, it's only fair that I share some of the expenses, Alec, so I want to pay for this."

"You don't have to do that, Henry. Dad's going to give me a regular allowance for the work I do around the house."

Henry smiled. "Sure," he came back, "and we're going to need all the money we can get—it takes money to make a champion, y'know. And we can't skimp on the Black's food. That's why we're going to have to work together just like partners. C'mon now, take this money and beat it down to the store." Henry shoved the money into the boy's hand.

Alec looked from the old jockey to the stallion. "Okay, partner," he said, smiling.

The next morning Alec went back to school. Whiff Sample and Bill Lee fell in beside him as he left the building at 12:30.

"What's all this about you bein' in a shipwreck and everything?" Whiff asked excitedly.

"Yeah, it was in the paper yesterday morning, and you even came home with a horse," Bill finished.

"It's the truth," Alec answered. "And if you don't believe me, come on along and I'll show him to you. I'm going over to the stable now."

"We sure will," they answered together.

When they reached the barn, Alec saw Henry. "Hello," he yelled.

"So you brought along some spectators, heh, Alec?"

Whiff's and Bill's eyes were turned toward the field where the Black grazed in a corner. "Gosh," they said.

The Black raised his head when he heard Alec's voice. His ears pricked forward and he whistled. Alec whistled back. Suddenly the horse broke toward them. Whiff and Bill hung back with Henry, as Alec walked toward the fence.

The Black hesitated when he saw the newcomers. He screamed and trotted back down the field. Henry didn't have to urge Whiff and Bill to move out of sight. They ran into the barn—their eyes wide with excitement. "Did you see him!" gasped Bill.

"Boy, he's the biggest horse I ever did see and what a mean look!" answered Whiff. They watched from the window of the barn.

The Black broke into a long, loping gait and ran toward Alec, as he walked into the field. "Better get back, Alec," yelled Henry. "If he doesn't slow up, he'll hit you."

The stallion thundered down upon the boy. Five yards away he swerved, barely missing him. He ran to the fence, turned and once again ran toward him. He swerved as he had done before. "Better get out of there, Alec," Henry warned.

"He just wants to play, Henry," Alec yelled over his

shoulder. "We did this all the time on the island! It's like a game of tag."

"Yeah," Henry called, "some fun!" He watched as Alec ran after the Black until he got him into a corner. The stallion reared and pawed the ground. He ran to one side, then to the other. Alec slowly approached him, both hands spread apart. The Black snorted, his long mane falling over his eyes. Suddenly Alec ran toward him. The stallion whirled and broke for the side. Alec reached out and slapped him on the hindquarters. The Black ran to the center of the field, then turned and looked back, shaking his head.

"What a pair!" Henry said to himself.

The stallion charged back at the boy, again swerving when he was almost on top of him. For ten minutes Henry watched the strangest game he had ever witnessed. And slowly he began to understand the strange understanding that had grown between this wild stallion and the boy.

A few minutes later Alec came up to him. His shirt was wet with sweat and his blue eyes glistened with excitement. "Do you see, Henry," he exclaimed, "he just wanted to play! Look at him, Henry—did you ever see anything so great in all your life?"

The Black had broken into a gallop and was running around the field. His mane flew back in the wind, and as he neared them his powerful strides shook the ground. He swept past. Henry didn't say anything until the stallion had come to a stop at the other end of the field, had whirled and looked back at them. Henry's own eyes were bright, too. "No," he said, "I've never seen anything like him—not even Chang.

"I wrote to my friend in the Jockey Club," he continued, after a moment's silence. "I explained the situation and asked if there wasn't some way we could check up on the Black's pedigree. He should be registered somewhere."

"How long before he'll answer you, Henry?"

"Should be sometime this week, telling us what to do, anyway."

"I hope so," Alec said. "It can't be too soon for me."

"Me, either. . . . Guess we'd better bring him in now; he's been out long enough. Then we'll make the fence a little higher in spots, so we won't be chasing him through the park like we did yesterday."

The boy whistled and the Black came running toward him. Alec grabbed him by the halter and rubbed his nose. He was leading him toward the barn when he heard someone shout, "Hey, Alec, keep away! Don't bring him in here! We're here!" The stallion snorted.

"What do you know, Henry, I forgot all about Whiff and Bill," Alec said. "They're still in the barn. . . . Come on out, fellows. I'll hold the Black here."

The two boys came out, a little sheepishly.

"Guess we'd better get home to lunch," Whiff said. They hurried down the driveway as the stallion screamed softly.

"Guess they believe me now," Alec said, grinning.

After dinner that same night, Alec went back to the barn. Tony had already stabled old Napoleon for the night. Alec saw him shove his white nose over into the Black's stall to steal some of his oats. The Black playfully nipped him, and Napoleon quickly withdrew his head. Alec couldn't get over the fancy the Black had taken to Napoleon. He wasn't afraid to leave him alone now, for as long as the old, gray horse was around, the stallion was quiet. A little later Alec bedded the Black's stall, turned out the lights and went home.

Days passed into weeks, weeks into months. And Alec's life, from the moment his alarm awakened him at five o'clock every morning until he closed his books at night, became as regular as a time clock. Always in the morning before school, he would feed, groom and ride the Black around the field. If the weather was nice, he would leave him outside, knowing Henry would be around to watch him. He didn't have time for games after school with the fellows any more. He had too many things to do. He would rush home at 12:30, as soon as his last class was over, eat lunch and then once again go to the stables where Henry was usually waiting for him.

Henry had received an answer from his friend in the Jockey Club, giving him the address of a Stud Book Registry Office in the Middle East. "It's very doubtful whether they can help you, though," he wrote, "as you have so little information to work on. However, I'm sure that they will do their best."

Henry wrote to them. "Now all we can do is wait and hope," he told Alec. "It will take a long time. That isn't going to stop us from training the Black, though. I want to put a watch on that fella—even if we aren't ever able to put him in a race!"

They hadn't attempted to put saddle or bridle on the Black yet. Henry wanted to wait until spring. The weather became cold and the ground hard.

"Our real work begins in the spring," Henry told Alec. "Now we'll just take it easy!" Under Henry's expert tutelage, Alec's riding skill became greater and greater until Henry nodded with approval. "A grand combination," he said to himself as he watched the boy ride high on the stallion's withers as he galloped down the field.

After the workouts, Alec would usually spend the rest of the afternoon doing the odd jobs around home which his father gave him. "Have to earn your allowance," his father said.

He had found plenty of things for him to do, too. Alec never had known there was so much to be done around a house—and his father hadn't missed up on a thing. The front and back porch gleamed with new paint. The garage doors now opened easily and stayed open. The cellar shone with cleanliness. And Alec never knew so many leaves could fall from trees. One day he would rake up and burn hundreds of them; the next day the yard would be covered again. Then with the coming of cold weather, there was work to be done in the house. Luckily enough, even though it was now January, snow hadn't fallen and the walks didn't have to be shoveled.

There was still no news about the Black's parentage.

"I'm afraid it's no use, Henry," Alec told him.

"Don't give up yet, son," Henry replied, but Alec could tell that he, too, had very little hope.

One afternoon, Alec walked toward the barn. The sky was overcast and the air cold. "Have to take it easy with him today," he thought. He pulled open the barn door. Henry sat in his favorite chair, tipped perilously back on two legs against the wall. He was looking at the Black, who was moving restlessly in his stall.

Henry turned as the boy closed the door. "Hello, Alec," he said.

"Hello, Henry. What's the matter with the Black?"

"He's all right," replied Henry. "Kept him in all morning, though, and he's pretty fidgety. The ground's pretty hard, and I didn't want him out there by himself. He'll feel better after you've given him a few turns around the field. Do your best to hold him down."

The stallion snorted and reached his head out toward Alec. Alec went over and placed a hand on his nose. "Hello, fella," he said. "Want to get some air, don't you?" The stallion shook his head.

"How's everything at school?" Henry asked.

"Managing all right, Henry. Made up most of my work, and things seem to be working out better than ever before. Guess it must be the regular hours," and he laughed.

"Yep," said Henry. "Keep it up, Alec, and we'll show your folks that you can raise a champion race horse and get good marks at the same time!"

Alec looked out the window. "Henry," he exclaimed, "look, it's snowing!"

The front legs of Henry's chair came down with a bang. He went to the window beside Alec. "Sure enough it is," he said. They watched the snow fall heavier and heavier. "Well, it's about time, anyway. Never seen it hang off so long before," he said.

"Yeah," said Alec glumly, "and I can just see myself shoveling tons of it off the walk!"

A regular blizzard started raging outside. "Sure is coming down," said Henry.

The Black was watching the snow, too. His eyes were wide with wonder, his ears pitched forward. "Henry," said Alec, "look at the Black. This is the first time he's seen snow!"

"That's right!" exclaimed Henry. "They don't have any where he comes from!"

"Wonder how he's going to react to it?"

"Shouldn't bother him any," answered Henry. The Black pawed the bedding of his stall.

"Seems pretty nervous," Alec said.

"Yep, but that's because he hasn't been out," replied Henry thoughtfully.

For the next half hour, Henry and Alec watched the falling snow. "Seems to be stopping now," said Alec.

A few minutes later the sun broke out of the clouds. "Certainly is beautiful out there now," said Henry as he and Alec watched the sun's rays glisten on the white snow.

The boy turned toward the Black. "Do you think we dare take him out, Henry?" he asked.

Henry looked at the stallion, who was still pacing his stall. "He sure needs the air, Alec. It's hard to keep a horse of his nature penned up, even for a day. Do you think you could manage him?"

Alec smiled. "I'm not afraid of anything with the Black, Henry—you know that," he answered.

Henry grinned. "Okay, let's get him out!" he said as he walked toward the stall.

As soon as Henry opened the stall door, the Black pushed his way out. Alec grabbed hold of his halter. "Whoa, Boy," he said.

Henry moved toward the barn door. "Better lead him around awhile until he gets used to it," he said as he pulled back on the door. The Black shied and Alec took a firmer grip on the halter. Cautiously he led the stallion out of the barn.

The air was cold and still. The Black's hoofs sank into the snow. He moved gingerly around the boy, never letting his feet remain more than a fraction of a second in the same spot. The snow flew in all directions. Slowly

Alec led the Black around the yard in front of the barn. The stallion kept shaking his head, and his breath shot from his nostrils, sending two streams of thick vapor into the air.

Alec attached the lead rope to the halter, giving him more room to run around. The stallion made a circle around him. Suddenly he stopped. Cautiously he lowered himself to the ground and then rolled over on his back. His legs waved above him.

"Look at him!" Alec shouted to Henry. "He loves it!"

After a few minutes, the Black climbed to his feet. Alec took him by the halter. "How'd you like it, fella?" he asked. The stallion shook his head. Alec laughed and brushed the snow off his back. "Okay to get on him now, Henry?" he asked.

"Sure," answered Henry. He walked over beside the Black and boosted Alec onto the stallion.

"Remember, take it as easy as you can," cautioned Henry, as Alec guided the Black into the field. He went at a fast walk, his legs sinking deeper and deeper into the snow.

Alec reached down and patted the Black's neck. "How do you like this, fella?" he asked again. The Black swerved a little and broke into a slow trot. Alec let him go and then drew him up into a walk again. "Take it easy, Boy," he said.

Now Alec let the Black go where he wanted to. He knew the stallion was enjoying the snow. He headed down into the hollow at the lower end of the field. The snow was a little deeper there. The stallion stepped high and once he rose a little on his hind legs. Alec guided him out of the hollow. The Black broke into a canter and Alec let him go, but kept a firm hand on him. The cold wind blew in his face and the snow went flying. When they reached the end of the field, he pulled the stallion up.

After an hour of riding, he saw Henry wave him in. He turned the Black toward the barn. "He liked the snow," he said when he came up to Henry.

"Sure looked that way," Henry said, grinning. "Wasn't as bad as I thought he'd be!"

Alec dismounted. "He's acting more like a gentleman every day," he said.

"Yep," said Henry, "and when spring rolls around he should be all ready for us to go to work on him."

"Spring," repeated Alec. "It isn't far away, Henry— just a few short months."

The man and boy looked at each other—both thinking the same thing. Henry's gaze shifted to the Black. "Maybe around the first of April, if all goes well," he said.

Training Begins

12

Alec's feet scraped beneath his desk. He fidgeted with the pencil in his hand. The paper in front of him was blank. He couldn't think about geometry at a time like this. His eyes again went to the clock on the side of the wall—12:15. Another fifteen minutes and he'd be on his way! His gaze shifted to the huge calendar hanging over the blackboard—April first! He had waited so long for that date, and now it was here. Today, after months of preparation, they were to break the Black to bridle and saddle, start the real training of the Black, even though no word had yet reached them from the Middle East concerning the stallion's pedigree. Henry had written two more letters in the last few months.

Alec saw the teacher looking at him, so his gaze dropped to the paper in front of him. The minutes crept by as slowly as all the months of waiting. He couldn't stand this much longer—he'd just have to go!

Suddenly the bell rang, and like a sprinter off on his marks, Alec leaped for the door. He had it opened and was out in the corridor before the rest of the class had started to move. He ran down the hall, heard an authoritative voice tell him to stop, but kept running. Nor did he stop when he reached the street. He ran until he was too tired to go farther, then slowed down to a fast walk.

He rushed into the house and threw his books on the couch. His mother had lunch ready. He sat down to eat, but he was too excited. He looked up at his mother. "I'm sorry, Mom, but I'm not hungry today," he said. His mother looked at him. She saw the high flush of excitement on his face.

"Something important going on?" she asked.

"Kinda, Mom," Alec answered as he finished a glass of milk. "I won't be home until dinner. I'll make up for my lunch then!" He ran out of the house. His mother stood in the doorway and watched him as he tore down the street.

Alec found Henry nervously pacing up and down in front of the barn. "Hello, Henry!" he called.

"Hello, son," Henry replied, taking the pipe from his mouth. "Nice warm day for it." He looked up at the sun high overhead.

Alec saw the stallion out in the field. "How does he feel today?"

"He's been pretty frisky all morning. Guess the warm weather is making him feel pretty good, too," answered Henry.

They watched the Black for a few minutes. Then Henry said, "Well, son, we might as well get started. Feel okay?"

"Sure. What's the difference riding the Black with a saddle or without one?"

Henry knocked the ashes from his pipe. "All depends on the horse, but let's get going. I picked up an old saddle in New York yesterday. It isn't so good, but it'll do the trick until we get him on a track and can use mine." Henry walked toward the barn.

Alec whistled. The Black raised his head and came trotting up to him. "Hello, fella." Alec put his hand on the stallion's neck.

The Black shoved his nose into Alec's side pocket. Alec playfully shoved him away and pulled a couple of lumps of sugar out of his pocket.

"Want some sugar, heh, Boy?"

The stallion swept his long, pink tongue over Alec's hand and the sugar disappeared.

Henry came toward them carrying the bridle and saddle. "Let's get over in the middle of the field where you'll have plenty of room."

"Okay," answered Alec. The Black trotted beside Alec. When they came to the center, Henry placed the bridle and saddle on the ground. "We'll try the saddle first," he said. "No telling what's going to happen."

Alec stood at the Black's head, a firm grip on the halter. Henry took the saddle in his arms and went around to the left side of the stallion. Alec saw the Black's eyes turn toward Henry. He sensed something was up and moved uneasily. Alec stroked him and spoke in his ear.

Henry said, "Hold him now, son."

Alec gripped the halter tighter. Henry raised the saddle over the Black's back and gently placed it on the stallion. He never got the chance to grasp the cinch. The stallion's hindquarters rose in the air and the saddle went flying. He turned nervously in a circle, and Alec had his hands full trying to hang on to him. Henry picked up the saddle and once again approached the Black. "This isn't going to be easy," he said, between clenched teeth. "Hold him again, Alec!"

Once again Henry placed the saddle on the stallion and once again it went flying in the air. "Doesn't give me a chance to tighten the cinch," he said as he picked it up.

Fifteen minutes passed and they still hadn't succeeded in getting the saddle on the Black. Henry and Alec were both tired. Yet the stallion wasn't as excited as Alec had expected him to be. "He's just being contrary," he told Henry.

The Black wouldn't leave the saddle on his back long enough for Henry to get the girth straps through the buckles. "If I could only some way get 'em through and tighten that saddle on him!" he said.

Alec thought a minute. "It's the cinch that bothers him. Let's lengthen it all the way on my side, then I'll hold the saddle just above his back while you get the end of the straps through the buckles. Once I drop the saddle, you tighten. You'll have to work fast. . . ."

"Might work," said Henry.

The Black moved nervously around. "Whoa, Boy," Alec said. He lowered the saddle as close to the stallion's back as possible, so Henry could get the straps into the buckles.

"All set, Henry?" Alec asked.

"Just a second," came the answer.

The Black was looking toward the far end of the field. Henry said in a low voice, "Okay, now."

Quickly Alec placed the saddle on the Black's back. The stallion reared. Alec jumped to one side. Henry was dangerously close to the Black, his hands feverishly pulling the straps through the buckles. Alec saw him give a final tug, then he flung himself out of the way of the Black's pawing hoofs. "Got it," he shouted. "Get out of his way!"

The stallion reared again and then raced down the field, swerving and throwing his hind legs in the air. He tried desperately to get rid of the saddle. Alec and Henry watched him as he plunged around the field. Suddenly the Black reared high on his legs and then fell over backward. They heard the saddle break.

"There it goes," said Alec.

"If he doesn't get it off, it'll be worth it!" answered Henry.

The Black finally climbed to his feet. The saddle was torn and broken, but still on his back. Again the stallion raced up the field, his excited eyes shifting from one side to the other. As he neared them, Alec whistled. The stallion swept past them. Alec whistled again. Suddenly the Black stopped, half-reared and turned. His ears pricked forward and he stood still for a few seconds. Then he was off again down the field, swerving and kicking.

"It's a good thing you were able to get that cinch tight, Henry!"

"Yeah," answered Henry, his eyes still following the Black.

Alec whistled again when the stallion came up the field. The Black stopped about thirty feet from them. Alec cautiously walked toward him.

"What's the matter, fella? Frightened of that saddle on your back?"

The stallion turned and Alec thought he was going to run down the field again. Instead he circled and then stood still. Alec put his hand in his pocket and drew out some sugar. He held it out toward the Black. "Here, Boy." Slowly he walked up to him and gave him the sugar. He stroked the long, sleek neck. "You'll get used to it, fella." He saw that the saddle was pretty well damaged but still usable.

"Walk him around a few minutes, Alec," Henry shouted.

Alec took the Black by the lead rope and started down the field. The stallion stepped lightly along, every once in a while throwing his hind legs in the air. Ten minutes later Alec led him back to Henry. "He isn't so bad now," he said.

"Hop on him then, and let's see what happens."

"Okay," answered Alec, moving toward the left side of the stallion.

Henry gave the boy a boost and he landed in the saddle. A fraction of a second later he found himself flying through the air. The ground rushed up at him. Alec managed to draw his feet up under him and break his fall. He lay still a moment, his body aching. Henry rushed over and knelt down beside him. "Hurt, son?" he asked anxiously.

"Guess not, Henry. Just a little jarred."

Henry ran his fingers over Alec's legs. "Try getting to your feet," he said. Alec pulled himself up. He was unsteady for a moment, and then his head began to clear. He saw the Black a few feet away. The stallion looked at him and then came forward. He pushed his nose into Alec's side pocket. "Seems just like old times on the island," Alec said. He turned to Henry. "Why does he throw me just because he has a saddle on his back?"

"Guess it's just one of those things, Alec. You never

know how a horse like this is going to act!" Henry answered. "He isn't used to the saddle yet, and I don't think he really knew you were on his back; all he could feel was that extra weight. Now this time talk to him like you always have before, let him know you're getting on—guess we sort of sneaked up on him then. Let him feel your arms and legs."

"Okay, Henry." Alec once again went to the Black's left side.

"Sure you feel all right?" Henry asked. "Want to wait a few minutes?"

"No," replied Alec. He looked at the stallion and held the halter with his two hands. "Now listen, fella, take it easy!" The stallion shook his head, almost taking Alec off his feet.

Alec kept talking into the Black's ear, and his hand ran up and down the stallion's neck. Then he was in the saddle! The black reared, but this time Alec was prepared. Up he went with the stallion high into the air, both hands grasping the Black's mane. The stallion came down and bolted across the field. Alec leaned forward and kept talking to him. The stallion's speed didn't slacken, and Alec thought he was in for another ride like the one on the island. Suddenly he found that he was able to guide the stallion—he had control of him. He turned him away from the fence and up the field again. They swept past Henry, and Alec shouted, "Okay!" The stallion didn't have room enough to run as fast as he wanted to, and after a short while, Alec managed to slow him down and bring him to a stop near Henry.

"Nice going, Alec," Henry said, gripping the Black's halter. "We'll put the bridle on him right away."

"But don't you think he's kind of tired, Henry?"

"That's one of the reasons why I want to do it now," Henry answered. "Besides, I don't think he's going to mind this as much as the saddle; it has a very light racing bit, and isn't much more than the halter he's got on now."

"You're the boss, Henry," Alec said. "How'll we do it?"

"You stay right on his back. I'll get the bit in his mouth, and then you can draw the bridle right over his head."

"Okay," Alec said, as Henry moved in front of the Black.

Henry's experienced hands had the bit in the Black's mouth within a few minutes. Alec quickly drew the bridle over the stallion's head. The Black shook his head and moved uneasily around in a circle. Alec let him alone. For fifteen minutes he let the Black get used to the bit, then he guided him down the field. Carefully, and in much the same manner as he had done back on the island, Alec taught the Black to turn right and left by a slight touch of the rein. There wasn't much difference between Alec's old way and the use of the reins, and the Black caught on quickly.

Alec rode back to Henry and dismounted. Henry smiled. "That, Alec," he said, "is what I call a good day's work."

"Sure is, Henry." Alec rubbed the Black's nose. "Nice going, Boy," he said proudly.

The sun was sinking behind Manhattan's skyscrapers in the distance as the man, the boy and the horse made their way back toward the barn.

Night Ride

13

Alec glanced at his wrist watch as he hurried away from the still-dark house where his mother and father were sleeping. One o'clock. It was two weeks since they had broken the Black to bridle and saddle. The full moon was high overhead; the stars were out; a warm spring breeze blew against his face. Henry would be waiting.

He reached the gate and let himself in. The truck Henry had borrowed was standing beside the barn. Henry was leaning against it.

"Everything all set, Henry?" Alec whispered.

"All set," came the quiet answer. He opened the barn door carefully so as not to make any noise. "Don't put on the light," he said over his shoulder, as Alec followed him inside.

The Black neighed when he heard them. Old Napoleon stuck his head out of his stall and neighed, too.

"Shhhh," said Alec and Henry together.

"Get over there and quiet them," Henry said. "I'll get the tack."

Alec put a hand on each of their noses. "Take it easy, boys," he said. "We don't want to wake anyone up, you know."

The horses recognized him now in the moonlight. The Black tossed his head gently; Napoleon brushed his long tongue around the boy's hand.

Henry returned, carrying the bridle and saddle. "Okay," he said. "Bring him out."

Alec led the Black out of his stall, without removing his blanket. The stallion stepped skittishly, his hoofs shaking the barn floor.

"Hey, Alec," Henry cautioned, "try to get him to stand still! He's going to wake the Missus sure as shootin'!"

"I'll try, Henry," the boy answered. "He seems pretty nervous, though; guess he isn't used to being awakened in the middle of the night!" The Black looked back at Napoleon and whinnied as Alec led him toward the barn door. Then Henry closed the door behind them.

Suddenly Napoleon neighed inside the barn—louder than either of them had ever heard him before.

"Jumpin' Jehoshaphat!" said Henry, as he ran toward the barn. "We'll never get out of here without waking someone up!"

The Black raised his head high in the air, his ears pitched forward, and he answered Napoleon's call. Alec looked at him, then at the barn.

"Henry," he said.

"Yeah."

"I've got an idea. Why not take Napoleon with us? The

two of them can fit into the truck—and I've a feeling it'll make the Black a lot easier to handle, besides being a lot quieter.''

Henry looked thoughtfully at the restless stallion. "Okay," he finally said. "It's worth trying." A minute later he led Napoleon toward the truck.

The Black neighed softly when he saw him, and Alec had no trouble getting him up the ramp into the truck. Henry followed with Napoleon. "Now," said Henry, "we not only have to get this moving van back to the guy I borrowed it from before six, but we have to get Napoleon back to Tony as well!"

"It's only one-thirty now," Alec said.

"We have to be over there by two." Henry climbed into the driver's seat and Alec sat beside him. A minute later the truck was moving down the driveway. Only the sound of hoofs came from the back of the van.

Henry drove rapidly through the darkened streets, and half an hour later they pulled up in front of a high iron gate. He touched the horn lightly twice. Over the gate Alec made out the name BELMONT. A glimpse of white caught his eye. Two hands grasped the bars, and a head topped with snow-white hair peered through.

"That you, Henry?" an aged high-pitched voice asked.

Henry leaned far out over the side of the car. "Yeah, Jake—it's me," he answered softly. "Everything okay?"

"Okay," came the answer.

Alec heard the rattle of keys, then the turning of the lock. A moment later the gate swung open. Henry put the car in gear and drove through. The gate was closed behind them. Henry didn't stop; he drove as if he knew his way around.

"Who was that, Henry?" Alec asked.

Henry kept his eyes on the graveled road in front of him, but Alec noticed a slight smile on his lips. "That's Jake," he answered. "We've been pals from 'way back. In fact," he grinned, "Jake taught me to ride. I was just a kid who loved horses and I wanted to ride, but I'd never even been on a horse. I used to go around and watch the early morning workouts, dreaming of the day when I'd be out there on some thoroughbred. Jake was a well-known jockey then—and I guess I sorta idolized him, but then all the kids did. Well, I guess Jake took me in hand just because he couldn't get rid of me. Anyway, he taught me 'most everything I know—and if I've been a success, he's the reason for it. Jake later went into training horses—and now he's sorta, well—retired, I guess you could call it."

Henry paused as he carefully turned a corner. Then he continued, "Y'know, Alec, horses are kind of like the sea, you'll find out—once you get used to 'em and learn to love 'em, you can't ever give them up. That's Jake and that's me. Jake's only the watchman around here now, but he loves it. There are horses training around here most of the year, and the track'll be opening up pretty soon, so he's content." Henry brought the truck to a stop beside the track.

"Are you sure no one's around, Henry?" Alec asked.

"Sure," answered Henry. "There are only a few horses in training and Jake's keeping an eye on them, so we practically have the place to ourselves."

Henry had pulled up beside an unloading ramp. They jumped out and went around to open the back doors. The horses whinnied as Alec climbed in beside them. The stallion threw back his head and tried to break free.

Alec grasped him by the halter. "Whoa, fella, take it

easy," he said. He backed the Black out onto the ramp and then down to the ground.

Henry followed with Napoleon. "It'll be a good thing to have Napoleon around where the Black can see him," he said. "Now you'd better walk the Black up and down a few times to get him loosened up."

"Okay," Alec said.

A few minutes later, when he walked the Black back toward the truck, he heard old Jake's high-pitched voice again and saw the little white-haired man talking to Henry. "Bejabers, Henry," he was saying, "don't tell me that gray imitation of a hoss there is the champion that I'm riskin' my job for!"

Henry laughed. "Bejabers yourself, Jake," he said. "Don't jump to conclusions so fast. You haven't seen this gray devil run yet."

"I'm too old a hand around here, my lad, for you to make me believe this critter can do anything but go around that track in a walk—bejabers, I am," Jake replied.

Alec couldn't help laughing. Jake heard him and turned. Then he saw the Black, and his mouth opened wide. Slowly he walked toward the stallion. The Black reared a little, but Alec quieted him down. Jake went around him, his eyes covering every inch of the Black.

Henry came up. "Well, Jake," he said, after a minute of silence, "what do you think of him?"

Jake looked up at him. "You sure were right, Henry. You've got a real horse here."

"Worth risking your job for?" Henry smiled.

"Worth risking my job for," the old man answered, nodding his head. "Haven't seen a horse like him"—he continued—"since Chang."

"That's just what I told Alec," Henry said. He winked at Alec. "Jake," he said, "meet the owner of this black stallion, Alec Ramsay—Alec, this is Jake."

Alec grasped the old man's hand in a warm clasp, and was surprised at the strength in Jake's fingers. "Glad to know you, son," Jake said.

"And I'm glad to know you, sir," answered Alec. "It was awfully nice of you to let us in here. Henry and I certainly appreciate it."

"Glad to do it," Jake replied. "Guess Henry knows my weakness. When he said you had a champion, I had to see for myself."

"You'll never change, Jake." Henry laughed.

"'Fraid not." The old man grinned.

The Black tossed his head, and the night breeze blew his mane. "He's rarin' to go, Henry," Alec said.

"Okay, I'll get the saddle." Henry moved toward the truck. "Stick around, Jake," he said over his shoulder, "and you'll see the fastest thing on four legs."

"Don't worry. I'm not a-goin'," Jake answered. "Come on, son." He turned to Alec. "We'll take him down near the gate."

A few minutes later Henry came up and threw the saddle on the Black. The stallion pranced easily, then reared a little when Henry tightened the cinch. Alec and Jake put the bridle on him.

"All set," Henry said, when they had finished. He turned to Alec. "Now the idea tonight, kid," he said, "is just to get him used to the track. Lucky there's a full moon so it isn't so dark out there, and I don't think you'll have any trouble seeing. Keep him under control as much as you can—try not to let him have his head until coming down the homestretch, then if everything is okay, let him out for a few hundred yards. I've been waiting a long while for this! Before you start, walk him down a ways and back. Got it?"

"Right," answered Alec.

Jake was leaning on the fence, his white head against the rail, his eyes on the stallion. He moved slightly and Alec saw the flash of silver in his hand. He knew Jake held a stopwatch.

Henry boosted Alec up on the Black's back and adjusted the stirrups. His knees came up, and he squatted on the small racing saddle like a veteran. The stallion moved uneasily. Henry led him out on the track.

"Okay, son," he said. "Walk him down and back first."

The Black stepped quickly over the soft dirt, his head high, his eyes shifting from side to side. Alec reached over and patted his neck. "Take it easy, fella," he murmured. The stallion wanted to run and Alec had his hands full keeping him to a walk. He went to the first turn and then came back. The night was warm, and as they approached Henry, Alec pulled off his sweater. "Save this till I come back." He tossed it to Henry, and walked the Black a few yards past him.

"Here goes," he said as he whirled the Black around.

The stallion reared. The boy clung to his neck, his white shirt standing out vividly against the Black's body. Then the stallion bolted forward. Alec tightened the reins and held him in. Down the track they streaked, the stallion's giant strides swallowing up the yards. Alec, high in his stirrups, hung low beside the Black's neck. The wind blew in his face and tears streamed down his cheeks. They swung around the first turn and into the backstretch. Alec kept him close to the white fence. He still held the Black in, but never before had he gone so fast, except on the island.

The stallion loved it and fought for his head. Alec tried frantically to hold him but, halfway down the backstretch, he got the bit in his teeth and ripped the reins out of the boy's control. Once again he was wild and free. Alec pulled on the reins with all his might, but the Black ran faster and faster. Alec couldn't see any more. The wind whipped him like a gale, tearing at his shirt.

As they rounded the far turn, the boy swayed in the saddle. Instinctively he clutched the Black's long mane and hung on for dear life. The stallion thundered into the homestretch. His legs were pounding the turf. They flashed past Henry and Jake, and then around the first turn they went again and once more into the backstretch.

Alec was weak from exhaustion. He tried to think. He had to stop the Black. He pulled desperately on the reins, but the stallion was once again on his own, running as he had been born to run.

It wasn't until they were halfway down the backstretch again that Alec felt the Black slow up just a little. Alec spoke into his ear; he loosened one hand from the mane and rubbed the stallion's neck. From then on his speed lessened gradually and, when they whipped by Henry again, Alec had him almost under control. He managed to slow him down after the first turn, and in the backstretch, Alec at last brought him to a stop.

He turned him around. The Black whistled and shook his head. He was breathing heavily, and a white lather covered his black body. He stepped lightly down the track toward Henry. A few minutes later Henry and Jake ran up to them, and Alec weakly climbed down from the saddle. Henry took the reins—they were sticky and wet with blood. He looked at Alec's bleeding hands, then gave the reins to Jake and put an arm around the boy to steady him. "Take it easy, son," he said.

"I'm all right, Henry," Alec said. "Just beat."

"After that ride you should be," Henry said.

"No one will ever be able to control this horse," Jake said. "Once he gets his head—only thing to do is what y'did, hang on and wait until he tires."

"I'll control him—one of these days," Alec said determinedly. He felt better now; strength was returning to his body and the earth was beginning to stand still. The stallion turned his head toward him, his ears pricked forward and he neighed softly. He shoved his nose against the boy.

Alec put a hand wrapped in a handkerchief against the soft muzzle. "You can't blame him, Henry," he said. "It's the first real fun he's had in a long, long time. I've just got to learn to stay on his back and enjoy the ride with him, that's all!"

"Yeah," said Jake, "that's all."

They walked off the track, Alec leading the Black. No one spoke again until they reached the truck. Napoleon stood there tied to the side. He raised his old, gray head curiously. Alec led the Black up to him and they put their heads together, the stallion obligingly lowering his.

Henry turned to Jake. "Guess you'll have to admit there isn't a horse in the country that can come close to him," he said.

Jake glanced down at the watch in his hand. "No," he

answered. "No, I've never heard of any horse doing the time he did tonight. Sun Raider and Cyclone would give him a race, but he'd beat them—if he ran."

"What do you mean—if he ran?" asked Henry.

Jake nodded toward the Black. "If he ever got on the same track with those horses, there'd never be any race. That horse would want to fight—not run. He's as wild as they come. Where'd you get him, son?" he asked.

Alec looked at Henry, who nodded. Alec told Jake briefly how he had acquired the Black.

When he had finished, Jake said, "Quite a story, son." Then he turned to Henry. "How do you know he's registered anywhere?" he asked. "You know as well as I do he can't run in any of the race meetings without bein' registered."

"Yeah, I know," Henry answered. "We're hoping he's listed in the Arabian Stud Book. I've been writing to them but they haven't answered—guess they can't find anything!"

Jake looked at the Black. "That horse was born wild, Henry. If I'm any judge—you'll never find him registered."

"I'm afraid you're right, Jake," Henry said, "but you never can tell, something might come up. We can race him against time and have him break a few records—then they'll have to notice him!"

Jake nodded. "Not a bad idea. Lots of people would give their right arm to see what I saw tonight!"

Alec walked the Black up and down for a while and then led him into the truck beside Napoleon. After tying the two horses securely, he jumped off the truck and went around to where Henry and Jake were talking.

Henry was saying, "We won't be around tomorrow night—give the boy a rest, but we'll make it the following night. Be at the gate by two o'clock."

"Okay," Jake answered.

Alec and Henry climbed into the front seat. Jake stood on the running board. Alec glanced at his watch. "Three-thirty," he said, as the truck started to roll. "Hope my folks haven't missed me."

"Yeah," murmured Henry, "and I hope the Missus hasn't missed *me* or there'll be plenty of explaining to do when I get home!"

Jake laughed and stuck his white head in through the window. "So she's still wearing the pants in the household, heh, Henry?"

"No, 'tain't that bad." Henry turned a corner sharply. "It's just that she's had enough of horses, and she expects me to be through with 'em too!"

"Then she still don't know you, does she?" Jake grinned. "You're like me, Henry," he continued, "as long as there's a breath left in your body, you'll want to be around horses and nothing in this world will keep you from 'em."

There was silence until the truck rolled up to the gate. Jake jumped off the running board and opened the gate. As it closed behind them, they waved good-bye to the old man.

"Well, son, you had a tougher time than either of us expected, didn't you?" Henry asked.

"Guess so, Henry," Alec answered, "but I'll be ready for him next time!" He relaxed in the seat and let his head fall back on the cushion behind him.

"Tired?" Henry asked.

"Kinda"—Alec tried to hide the weariness in his voice—"even in spite of that nap I took this afternoon. Mother couldn't understand it—said it was the first time she'd seen me in bed during the afternoon since I was four!"

"Guess you'll have to keep doing that for a while, Alec. I've fixed it up with Jake to go over there about three nights a week. You see, we have to take advantage of the time that we have now, before the track opens up for the season. There'll be too many horses and people around then to risk going in. I don't want to let anyone know about the Black until he races—that is, except Jake; we can trust him."

"If he *does* race," Alec said soberly. "We should've had a letter by this time if he's registered at all!"

"Aw, you never can tell," Henry answered. "They're pretty slow over there, y'know, and then there's probably a lot of things they have to look up."

"Yeah," Alec agreed sleepily. He curled his legs underneath him. "Anyway," he continued, "it's pretty exciting just riding the Black like I did tonight on a track."

"Yeah, and I must say you and the Black did a pretty good job. Made the track record look like it was made by a hobbyhorse!"

Fifteen minutes later they pulled up in front of the barn. Alec led the Black into his stall. Henry stabled Napoleon and then followed Alec into the Black's stall. Together the boy and the man rubbed him down.

A few minutes later they left the darkened barn.

"Good night, Henry," Alec said. "See you tomorrow."

"'Night, Alec."

The Ramsay house was still dark. Alec opened the door

carefully and climbed the stairs to his bedroom. All was quiet except for an occasional snore from his father.

Wearily he undressed and climbed into bed—his body aching.

A few hours later the alarm clamored in his ear. Half-consciously he reached for it and turned it off. A sharp pain in his hand drove all the sleepiness from him. He sat up and looked at the blood-stained handkerchief still wrapped around his hand. He let his head fall back against the pillow. Then it hadn't been a dream! He *had* ridden the Black last night! His eyes rested on the chair beside his bed where he had thrown his clothes. Hanging on the arm was his shirt—ripped by the wind.

His body still ached all over as he threw the blankets off and climbed out of bed. Quickly he dressed and tucked the torn shirt underneath his arm—he would throw it away before his mother saw it. He went into the bathroom, washed and took care of his cut hands. He clenched his teeth as he poured iodine on his hands—but his head was feverish with excitement.

*Cyclone
and Sun Raider*

14

Two nights later Alec once again rode the Black out on the track. The stallion tugged on the reins as Alec walked him. Henry and Jake leaned on the fence; Napoleon stood beside them, his eyes on the Black.

Alec wore a tight, black sweater; leather gloves covered his cut hands. He had his handkerchief tied around his head to keep the hair out of his eyes. The stallion half-reared and pulled on the reins—he wanted to run! Alec hunched closer to the Black's neck, his heart pounding, for he, too, wanted to feel the wind stream in his face again and feel the mighty stallion in action!

Suddenly he let loose on the reins and the stallion bolted. He gained momentum in mighty leaps. Faster and faster he went until once again the landscape became a blur, and only the endless line of white fence was there to guide them. Alec didn't attempt to hold the stallion.

"Run, run!" he yelled, but the tearing wind blew the words back down his throat.

Around the track they whipped, and Henry and Jake both pushed the stems of their stopwatches down as the Black streaked by. Eagerly they looked at the time and then at each other. "Never thought it possible," Jake said.

Their eyes turned again to the black blur rounding the turn. "Look at that horse run!" exclaimed Jake.

"Yeah—and look at that boy ride!" Henry shouted.

Jake's head rested on his hands against the fence. "I never knew a horse could have that much endurance, Henry," he said.

"Remember he's an Arabian."

"Not all Arabian, though, Henry—too big, too much speed. The blood of a good many horses runs in his veins. Yep, and only his love for the boy keeps him on that track now."

High in the stirrups Alec hung close to the Black's neck—it was like flying. Tears from the wind raced down his cheeks in an endless stream. Suddenly as they approached Henry and Jake, Alec saw the gray form of Napoleon lope out onto the track. They whipped by him. But the Black had seen Napoleon, too, and his speed slackened.

Alec glanced over his shoulder and saw the old gray horse running toward them. Gradually the Black slowed down, and then without waiting for a signal from Alec, whirled and galloped back toward the plodding Napoleon. The old horse wheezed as they came up to him, but he held his head high. He reached his nose up to the Black's, and then broke out into a trot and headed for the turn. The stallion whirled—three mighty leaps and he was up alongside him. Napoleon took three steps to every one of the Black's. Together they rounded the turn. Napoleon trotted ponderously, his eyes straight on the track ahead of him. The stallion shook his head and playfully nipped the gray horse. Three-quarters of the way around, Napoleon's pace slackened to a very slow trot.

When they reached Jake and Henry, Napoleon was exhausted, but his eyes were wide with excitement. Alec jumped off the stallion's back. "Now we've got two racers." He laughed.

"Don't know what got into him," said Henry. "Just tore off his halter and loped right out there when he saw the Black coming down!"

Jake rubbed his hand over Napoleon's body. "Guess he isn't any the worse for it," he said.

Henry threw the blanket over the Black. "Tony'll probably be wondering why he takes it so easy on his rounds tomorrow."

"He'll have more pep than ever." Alec laughed. "Tony will be lucky if he can hold him in!"

Jake threw another blanket over Napoleon. "Here," he said, "he earned this."

"Better walk 'em both down the track, son," Henry said.

Alec led the horses away. Napoleon raised his head as high as he could, imitating the Black. Carefully he raised his trembling legs higher and tried desperately to rear in spite of Alec's hand on his halter.

Henry and Jake were standing in front of the truck when Alec returned with the two horses. The two men looked at the stallion. "I'd give a lot to be able to spring him in a big race," Henry said. "Boy, what a sight that'd be!"

Alec looked at Henry. "We're not going to give up hope yet, Henry, are we?"

Henry's eyes swept up to the stallion and then back to Alec. "No, sir, kid, they're going to see this horse run if I have to stage a race myself!"

Henry lit his pipe. In the glow of the lighted match, Alec saw determination written all over his face. His jowls rose and fell as he sucked on the pipe; the thick smoke rose in the air and then floated away on the warm, spring breeze. Henry lifted the pipe from his mouth and turned to Jake. "Got any suggestions on anything we could do, Jake?"

The old man thought a minute. Then he said, "No, Henry. Guess the best thing to do is to race him against time some way and get people talkin' about him. But first I'd wait for the answer to your letter."

The stallion's ears pricked forward as a horse's neigh reached them from one of the stalls in the distance. Alec looked at the Black wistfully. "That's the way I feel about it, too, Henry," he said. "We'll wait, but he belongs up with the best, and some way we've got to show everyone that he does, thoroughbred or no thoroughbred!"

Weeks passed, and Alec and Henry conscientiously trained the Black. Eagerly they awaited an answer to Henry's last letter. The days passed and gradually they began to lose hope. Then one day it came. Henry rushed into the barn with the long, unopened envelope in his hand. Alec was grooming the Black.

"Alec," he yelled excitedly, waving the letter. "It's here!" Furiously his hands tore it open and the envelope fell to the floor.

Alec saw his eyes fly over the letter and then disappointment appeared on his face. He handed the letter to

Alec. It was short, only a few lines. Even then, Alec didn't read all of it. The first sentence was enough. "There is no horse registered to fit the description you sent us. We made an extensive search . . ." Alec handed the letter back to Henry, who crumpled it up and threw it on the floor.

In the days that followed, Alec showed his disappointment plainly. His night rides on the stallion were still as exciting as ever, but he longed to race the Black against the great race horses of the day.

He read every word the newspapers printed about them. Out in front fighting for top honors were the two greatest horses, turf experts said, that ever set foot on any track—Sun Raider and Cyclone. Sun Raider, the champion of the West Coast, winner of the Santa Anita Handicap, the biggest, fastest horse in racing, the reports from the Coast said. Cyclone was the pride of the East, Kentucky born and bred, winner of the Derby, the Preakness, the Belmont—no horse had ever pushed him to see what he could actually do. When that time came, his followers said, Cyclone's speed would astound the racing world.

Sports writers wrote long accounts of the two horses, prophesying what would happen if the two champions ever met. "If Sun Raider comes east, he'll push Cyclone to a new world's record," eastern reporters wrote. And the western reporters retaliated—"If Sun Raider ever goes east, he'll make Cyclone look like a mild summer breeze!"

Race after race passed into turf history. Sun Raider and Cyclone were the names on every person's lips. Men and women who had never seen a race argued over the merits of the two horses, and who would win, when and if they ever met. And all the time Henry and Alec looked at the Black and smiled grimly, for they knew they had a horse that could beat them both!

One Saturday morning a few weeks later, Alec rushed up to the barn with a newspaper in his hand. The Black at the far end of the field heard him and galloped past Henry. "Hello, fella!" Alec greeted him, as the stallion thundered to a stop and shoved his nose against him. Then Alec handed Henry the newspaper. "Read Jim Neville's column," he said.

Henry took the paper and turned to the famous sports reporter's column. "It is needless to say," he read, "that the greatest excitement in the sports world today is being caused by two of the fastest horses ever to set foot on any track, Cyclone and Sun Raider. Thousands of words have been written about these two champions during the last year, yes, and thousands of battles have been fought (off the track) as to just which one is the best. The irony of it all is that in most probability these horses will never meet. Mr. C. T. Volence, owner of Sun Raider, is not going to send his horse east this summer for any of the races here, and Mr. E. L. Hurst, owner of Cyclone, is not sending his horse west. It seems to me that both Mr. Volence and Mr. Hurst are failing in their duties as true American sportsmen. For here is a race that the whole nation is clamoring for, and whatever personal reasons these two gentlemen have for not wanting to bring these two horses together should be cast aside for the good of American racing.

"So I would like to suggest a match between Cyclone

and Sun Raider to be held in Chicago the middle of next
month. I'm sending letters to each of the owners today.
There are no big races at that time in which the horses
are entered. Both horses will have the same distance to
travel for the race, so neither will have any advantage
over the other.

"Once and for all the question of which horse is the
faster will be settled. . . ."

Henry looked up from the paper. "It will be a great
race if they let 'em run," he said.

The stallion stood quietly beside Alec, his big teeth
crunching on the sugar the boy had just given him.

Two days later as Alec walked home from school, he
passed a newsstand. The headline of a morning paper
leaped up at him—CYCLONE AND SUN RAIDER TO RUN
MATCH RACE JUNE 26! he read. Eagerly he bought a
paper and turned to Jim Neville's column.

The owners of the two champions had accepted his
proposal—the race was on! "Mr. Volence and Mr. Hurst
even went me one better," Jim Neville wrote. "They
have offered to give over their share of the purse money
to a worthwhile charity! I owe them both an apology, for
they are true sportsmen in every sense of the
word. . . ."

Alec couldn't get home and through lunch fast enough
to hear what Henry thought about it. When he reached
the barn, he saw Henry already had a paper and was
reading it. He looked up as Alec approached. "Well,
they've gone and done it!" he said.

"Boy, and I'd give a lot to see it!" answered Alec.

A car turned into the driveway. "Wonder who this is?"
asked Henry.

"It's Joe Russo—haven't seen him since he gave us that write-up the day we got home!" Alec exclaimed as the car neared them.

Joe jumped out. "Hello, Alec. Hello, Mr. Dailey. I was over this way covering a story and thought I'd drop in and see how you were doin' with that wild stallion of yours."

"He's okay now." Alec grinned proudly.

"Still keeps us on our toes, though," Henry said. "There he is out in the field now." He pointed to the Black.

Alec whistled. "I'll give you a closeup of him, Joe," he said.

The stallion ran toward them. He reared when he saw Joe, and rushed down the field again. "Guess he's forgotten me." Joe laughed.

Alec whistled again and the Black whirled and came back. Alec grabbed him by the halter.

"Boy! I knew I wasn't seeing things that night—he sure is the biggest horse I've ever seen!" Joe whistled admiringly.

"Fastest horse you've ever seen, too," said Alec proudly.

"Faster than Sun Raider and Cyclone?" kidded Joe.

"Beat both of 'em," Henry said.

Joe laughed. "Say, you guys sound serious! Here people all over the country are arguing about who's the fastest horse in the country—Sun Raider or Cyclone, and you say your horse can beat them both. Better not let anyone hear you say it!"

"It's the truth, Joe," Alec said. "We've been racing——" He stopped and looked at Henry.

"It's all right, Alec," Henry said. "Guess it doesn't

make much difference now who we tell; we can't race him anyway."

Joe looked from Alec to Henry. "You mean to tell me you've been racing him?"

"In a way," Alec answered. "We've been taking him over to Belmont at night and giving him some workouts."

"And let me tell you, sir," Henry broke in, "no horse ever ran around that track like this fellow did. We clocked him; there wasn't any guesswork."

"You see," Alec said, "we had planned to run him in some big races. I was going to ride—but we weren't able to get his pedigree. We wrote to Arabia trying to get it, but it was impossible. We didn't know much about him, only the port where he got on the boat. And you can't run a horse in a race without his being registered."

"Yeah, that's right," muttered Joe, "and while the Black looks like a thoroughbred, he is certainly too wild to have ever been brought up like one!"

"I guess that just about washes us up as far as racing goes, but we still know he's the fastest horse around!" Henry said.

Joe scratched his head. "You're sure he's as fast as you say he is?" Joe asked.

"Sure, I'm sure," replied Henry. "Why?"

"Well, I know of one race that he wouldn't need to be registered for."

"Some county fair?" Henry laughed.

"No—the match race between Sun Raider and Cyclone!"

"But that's impossible," Henry said.

"Nothing is impossible these days," Joe said. "But whether we could get him in or not, it wouldn't be his lack of registration papers that would keep him out. You see, that's a special match race—it isn't held at any race meeting. It's just like me racing you to see which one of us can run faster. They rent the track, bring the horses and away they go! All you have to do is get the other owners to let you run the Black in the race!"

"Yeah, that's all," Henry said, "and I still say it's practically impossible!"

"There's a slim chance, though, Henry," Alec said eagerly.

"You said it, kid." Joe grinned.

"How do you think we could work it, Joe?" Henry asked.

"I dunno—but you know I work on the same paper with Jim Neville, and he's the guy that started all this; he might help us some way."

"Perhaps if you told him about the Black . . ." suggested Alec.

"Maybe," answered Joe. "He's crazy about horses, and doesn't think that there's any horse in the world that can beat Cyclone, even Sun Raider. He'd probably think I was nuts if I told him I knew of a horse that could beat 'em both." He paused. "You're *sure* that the Black can?"

Henry smiled. "Yeah, Joe, I'm sure," he said, "but seeing that you're kinda skeptical, why don't you come over some night when we run him? Sure, and bring Jim Neville along, too; then he *will* have something to write about!"

"Not a bad idea, Henry," Joe answered. "I'll get in touch with Jim this afternoon. When you going to run the Black again?"

"Tomorrow night," Alec answered.

"If you can make it, you can meet us at the main gate at two o'clock," Henry said.

"Say, this is just like a mystery novel," Joe said, as he walked toward his car. "But I'll be there, and I have a feelin' Jim will too! So long!"

"So long," Alec and Henry called. The stallion raised his head and whinnied as the car rolled down toward the gate.

The Mystery Horse

15

The following night when Alec and Henry drove up to Belmont's main gate, they saw Joe's car parked there. Two men were inside. "That fellow with him must be Jim Neville," Alec said hopefully.

Henry brought the truck to a stop and lightly touched the horn. "Leave your car here," he called softly to Joe. "Jump on the truck—we've only a short way to go."

The two men climbed out of the car and leaped onto the truck's running board. Henry put the truck in gear as he saw Jake swing the gates open. Joe pushed his head in the open window near Henry. "Made it," he said. "Where do we go from here?"

"Hold tight, my friend. You'll find out," Henry said.

Five minutes later they came to a stop beside the track. Henry and Alec climbed out. A tall, broad-shouldered man stood beside Joe; his hat was shoved back off his forehead and Alec saw long streaks of gray running through his black hair. Somehow Jim Neville looked just as Alec had imagined he would. Joe introduced them.

After the introductions, Jim said, "Frankly," and his eyes squinted quizzically, "it's only the newspaper man in me that gets me out here tonight, because as much faith as I have in my pal Joe here, I can't imagine any horse in racing—today anyway—that can match strides with Cyclone or Sun Raider!"

Henry smiled. "Sure," he said, "I'd say the same thing if I hadn't seen the Black run!"

Jim Neville looked questioningly at Henry. "Say, you're not by any chance the same Henry Dailey who rode Chang to victory in all those races about twenty years ago, are you?"

"Sure he is!" Alec said proudly.

Jim Neville pulled his hat down over his forehead. Alec could see that once again he was the reporter on the scent of a story. "And you believe," Jim said seriously, "that you've got a horse here that can beat both Sun Raider and Cyclone?"

"Yep," Henry answered. "It's Alec's horse; I just help train him."

Joe Russo spoke up. "Why not show him the Black, Henry, and then we'll let him draw his own conclusions?"

"Good idea," said Alec, as he walked toward the back of the truck.

He led the Black out on the ramp. "Say," he heard Jim exclaim, "he is a giant of a horse!" The stallion shook his head. He was full of life tonight for he knew well that he was going to run. His small, savagely beautiful head turned toward the group of men below him. He drew up, made a single effort to jump, which Alec curbed, and then stood quivering while the boy talked soothingly and patted him.

Jake came up and Henry introduced him to Joe and Jim. "Say," Jake smiled, "this is growin' into quite a shindig, isn't it?"

Jim walked carefully around the stallion.

"Watch out. He might kick, if you get too close," warned Alec. "He doesn't know you."

"Don't worry! I won't get too close to this fellow," Jim said. "I'm beginning to see what you fellows mean," he added. "If he can run as well as he looks——"

Henry disappeared into the truck and came out leading Napoleon.

"Hey, what've you got here—another champion?" Jim threw back his head and howled.

"This is Napoleon." Henry grinned.

"He has sort of a quieting effect on the Black, so we always bring him along," Alec explained.

Jim Neville watched as Napoleon reached his nose up toward the stallion's. "Maybe not such a bad idea, after all," he said.

A few minutes later they boosted Alec into the saddle. The Black pawed the ground. Jim Neville got too close and the Black's teeth snapped as he tried to reach him. Henry held him back. It was plain to see he wasn't used to seeing so many people around at one time. He tossed his head up and down, his heavy mane falling over his forehead. Suddenly he rose on his hind legs, tearing the bridle out of Henry's grasp; his legs struck out, hitting Henry in the arm.

Alec pulled hard on the reins and jerked him to the side. "Black!" he said. "Down!" The men retreated quickly to a safe distance. Jake was rolling up Henry's sleeve, which was wet with blood.

"Did he get you bad, Henry?" Alec asked.

Jake and Henry were inspecting the wound. "Nothing broke," answered Jake. "Just a bad cut; we'll go up to the First Aid Room and fix it!"

"No, we won't," Henry said. "I came down here to watch this workout and I'm going to see it. I'll take care of this later—you gotta take more'n a cut in this business."

"He sure is a devil!" Jim Neville yelled from the other side of the Black.

"We got him excited, that's all," answered Henry. "First time he's done that to me."

Again the stallion reared and Alec brought him down. "Get him out on the track, kid," Jake yelled.

The Black pranced nervously as they went through the gate. Once again Alec felt his body grow warm with excitement. He patted the crest on the stallion's neck. "We're off, fella," he said. Alec looked back at the small group of men behind him. They were all leaning on the fence, watching eagerly.

Joe Russo's voice drifted toward him. "That kid's not going on any picnic," he said.

Alec grasped the reins still tighter and leaned over until his head touched the stallion's. He knew full well the danger that was his every time he rode the Black, especially when he let him loose on the track. The stallion would never hurt him knowingly, but once he got his head he was no longer the Black that Alec knew—but once again a wild stallion that had never been clearly broken, and never would be!

Suddenly the Black bolted. His action shifted marvelously as his powerful legs swept over the ground. Fleet hoofbeats made a clattering roar in Alec's ears. The stallion's speed became greater and greater. Alec's body grew numb, the terrific speed made it hard for him to breathe. Once again the track became a blur, and he was conscious only of the endless white fence slipping by. His fingers grasped the stallion's mane and his head hung low beside his neck. His only thought was to remain on the Black's back and to stay alert. His breath came in short gasps, the white fence faded from his vision; desperately he tried to open his eyes, but his lids seemed held down by weights. Bells began to ring in his ears. Alec's fingers tightened on the Black's mane. He lost all track of time—then the world started turning upside down.

It seemed hours later that he felt arms reach around his waist. Then the next thing he knew, he found himself lying flat on his back beside the truck. He looked up at the men grouped around him. Henry knelt beside him, his white handkerchief stained with large dark spots bulging around his arm. Alec's eyes fell to his own hands. Strands of long, black hair were clenched between doubled fists. Questioningly he looked up at Henry.

"How——" he began.

"It's all right, kid. You wouldn't let go of him. Feel all right?"

"Kinda dizzy," answered Alec. "Where's the Black?"

"He's okay—we put him in the truck with Napoleon."

"Did I fall off, Henry?" Alec asked.

Jake's high-pitched voice reached Alec's ears. "Fall off?" he said. "Boy, if that hoss was still running, you'd still be on him. Took all of us to get you off his back when he did stop, and then Henry was the only one of us who could get near him."

"I'm glad I stuck on him," Alec said. "Y'know, Henry, we've never seen that horse run his fastest yet. I just couldn't seem to breathe that time."

"Takes courage to ride him, kid," Henry answered. "I'm pretty proud of you, but let's try getting you to your feet. Better for you if you can walk around."

Alec swayed a little as Henry and Jake lifted him up, but gradually the earth stopped turning around and his brain cleared. He breathed in the night air deeply.

Jim Neville came up. "Kid," he said, "I've seen a lot of riding in my day, but never any to equal that!" Jim then turned to Henry. "You were right, Mr. Dailey—he is the fastest horse we've ever seen. I can hardly believe what I saw with my own eyes but"—Jim held the face of a stopwatch up in front of Henry—"I can't deny this!" Then he turned brusquely to Joe Russo. "And now, Joe, we both have a deadline to make, so let's get going."

"Right, Jim."

"Come around again—anytime you want," Henry urged, "and we'll let you see the grandest animal on four feet run without even charging admission."

Jim Neville's eyes twinkled. "A lot of people are going to see that horse in action if I have anything to say about it!" he said.

Alec felt the earth whirl around him again. "Honest, Jim," he said, "do you think we could?"

"I'm not promising anything, kid," replied Jim, "but I'm going to start something or I miss my guess. Take a look at my column tomorrow. And now we do have to get going. Come on, Joe."

"I'll go along with you and let you out," said Jake.

After they had gone, Henry put his arm through Alec's and they walked back and forth until the blood once again was circulating through the boy's legs. "I feel okay now, Henry," he said.

They climbed into the truck. Alec looked back through the small window, and saw the stallion peering anxiously at him. "Yep, mister," he said, "that was quite a ride!"

"Well, Alec," Henry said, "I hope that whatever Jim Neville is going to do gets us in that race."

"You're not hoping any more than I am."

The next day was Saturday. Alec rushed over to the barn immediately after breakfast. Henry always had a morning paper and probably he was already reading Jim Neville's column.

Sure enough, he was sitting outside reading as Alec came up. "What's he say?" the boy asked anxiously.

Henry grinned as he handed him the paper. "Read it for yourself."

Alec's eyes swept over the headline—WHO IS THE MYSTERY HORSE THAT CAN BEAT BOTH CYCLONE AND SUN RAIDER? "Yes, I know," Jim Neville wrote. "I'm the guy that said there wasn't a horse in the world that could beat that rarin' red bundle of dynamite—Cyclone. Not even Sun Raider. Yep, and I'm the guy that wrote to Messrs. Volence and Hurst, owners of these thorough-breds, suggesting the coming match between their horses on the twenty-sixth of June—just two weeks off.

"This race in my mind—and I suppose in the minds of the whole American public—was to settle one thing: To see which horse was the fastest in the country! Both Cyclone and Sun Raider had beaten everything they had met on the track, and it was only natural then that they should meet to settle this question of track supremacy.

"But now, in my mind, this race will no longer prove

who's the fastest horse on four legs, because I've seen a horse that can beat both of them. This is something I have to get off my chest, because you racing fans are going to crown the winner of Chicago's match race as the world's fastest horse—and it isn't true. There is still another horse—a great horse, who can beat either one of them.

"It's only fair to tell you that this horse has never raced on a track, and perhaps never will—because he lacks the necessary registration papers. And now I find that I'm coming to the end of my column, so I'll close with just this reminder that while you folks are acclaiming the winner of the coming Cyclone–Sun Raider race as today's champion, I know of a horse—a mystery horse that's right here in New York—who could probably make both of them eat his dust!"

"Say, that *is* starting something," said Alec.

"You said it, son; he'll have everybody on his neck before this day is out!"

"He didn't come right out and suggest that the Black run in the match race, though, Henry," Alec said.

"No—but he's left the door wide open and you can bet somebody will suggest it."

"Gee, I hope it works, Henry. Just think, the Black against Cyclone and Sun Raider. Boy! What a race!"

"You said it!" Henry agreed. Then he paused for a minute. "Say, Alec, wonder if we did get the Black in the race—how do you think your folks would take it? About you ridin', I mean."

Alec's eyes met Henry's. "They just gotta let me ride, Henry. They'll understand, I'm sure, especially after we tell them how I've been riding the Black at Belmont. Funny thing, Henry—Mother decided last night that she's going to Chicago middle of next week to visit my aunt for a couple of weeks. She'll be there at the same time as the match race!"

"Whew," said Henry, "that's somethin'!"

"Mother isn't interested in races; she probably won't even go to see it! You know, Henry, as long as we don't even know yet whether the Black is going to be in the race, I won't even mention it to Mother. If the Black does get in—I'll talk it all over with Dad; he'll understand."

"Hope so," answered Henry.

When Alec looked over the evening papers that night, he saw that Henry certainly was right about everybody's jumping on Jim Neville's neck. The sport pages were filled with articles ridiculing Jim's "insane idea" that there was a horse in America—yes, right here in New York—that could beat the two champions!

Because Jim Neville's column was carried in papers from coast to coast, and because he was one of the foremost sports authorities in the country, his articles on the mystery horse aroused more and more curiosity with every day that passed. And in spite of the criticism that he was getting, Jim wouldn't let the public forget about his mystery horse. Each day in his column he would carry a paragraph about him. Each night on his network sports program, he would again mention him.

One sports writer wrote, "Only a figure as well-known as Jim Neville could have created such a hullabaloo as is now going on over the merits of a mystery horse that Neville claims can beat both Sun Raider and Cyclone!"

A week passed and the small snowball that Jim had started rolling continued to gain momentum. "Who is this mystery horse?" the racing public wanted to know. Jim's only reply was that he had promised to keep his name a secret, but that he could get him at a moment's notice.

He called Henry and Alec on the telephone. "Don't run him at Belmont any more," he told them. "This is getting bigger than I had even hoped it would. We'll have the Black in that race yet!"

Another week passed. Alec's mother left to visit her sister in Chicago. The match race was only one week off.

Alec felt a little discouraged as he made his way toward the barn early one morning to give the Black a workout before he went to school. Time was growing short—if they only had another two weeks . . .

He met Tony coming out of the barn with Napoleon.

"Hello, young fella," he said. "Ah, thees is da life." He pounded his short, stocky arms against his chest and breathed in the early morning air.

"Yeah," Alec said. "Sure is, Tony."

Tony backed Napoleon into his wagon and started harnessing him up. "What's-a da matter, young fella? You look kinda down in da dumps."

"I'm all right, Tony," Alec answered. "Guess I was just thinking."

"Too much-a thinkin' doesn't do nobody good," Tony said wisely as he climbed into the seat.

"Guess you're right, Tony. See you later."

"You betcha," came the reply.

Alec led the Black out of his stall and went over him with a soft cloth. Then he snapped the long lead rope on his halter and led him out into the early morning sunshine. The stallion ran around the boy, kicking his heels high into the air. Then he came closer and playfully tried to nip Alec. "Feeling pretty good this morning, aren't you?" Alec asked.

A few minutes later he threw the saddle on him and

rode him into the field. Somehow he always felt different when he was astride the Black. It was like being in a world all his own. Forgotten were his problems, the city around him—it was like flying in the clouds.

A half-hour later he slipped down from the stallion's back and led him back into the barn. He had just finished feeding him when Henry came in. "I'm almost late for school, Henry," Alec said. "Would you mind giving him the once-over with the cloth——?" He stopped as he saw a wide grin on Henry's face.

"Sure," Henry said, "but read this before you go, lad!" He handed Alec the morning paper.

Alec turned quickly to Jim Neville's column. His heart seemed to stop when he read the headline: MYSTERY HORSE TO RUN IN CHICAGO MATCH RACE. He swelled all up inside, and for a minute he couldn't see the paper—then it became clear again.

"Yesterday," Jim Neville wrote, "I received one of the most sporting letters that I have ever had the pleasure to receive. It was from Mr. E. L. Hurst, owner of Cyclone. His letter was short and to the point. He suggested that since the match race to be held in Chicago next week is just for the good of racing and the proceeds are all going to charity, he saw no reason why my mystery horse should not run against his horse and Sun Raider. Mr. Hurst said that he sincerely believed that Cyclone had never been pushed as fast as he could go, and there was no horse on earth that he feared. If the owner of the mystery horse believed that his horse could beat Cyclone, he would not object to his trying as long as it was also satisfactory to Mr. C. T. Volence, owner of Sun Raider.

"As soon as I received Mr. Hurst's letter, I phoned

Mr. Volence in Los Angeles and read it to him. I asked him if he felt the same way about it, and he said, 'Yes, definitely.' He went on to say that, with the country talking so much about this mystery horse, it would save them running another match race next month. 'Might as well kill two birds with one stone—' he said, 'Cyclone and Neville's Folly!'

"Neville's Folly, heh, Mr. Volence—just wait'll you see him in action!" the article finished.

Alec looked up from the paper at Henry. Slowly a grin spread over his face. Instead of feeling delirious with excitement as he had expected, he felt cool and composed.

"He's in, Henry," he said. "He's in!" The man and the boy looked at each other, and then turned and walked toward the stallion, who had stuck his black head out the stall door and was looking at them curiously.

Preparation

16

Alec never knew how he got through the rest of that day in school. All that he could think of was that a week from today he'd be racing the Black against Cyclone and Sun Raider! Somehow, he still couldn't believe that all this was happening to him—Alec Ramsay.

That night after dinner, he walked into the living room where his father was reading. He sat down in a chair and nervously turned the pages of a magazine. His father looked up from his paper.

"Received a letter from Mother today, Alec. She's getting a big kick out of Chicago and seeing your aunt again. Says if everything is okay here, she'll stay three weeks. That all right with you?"

"Sure, Dad." Alec smiled. "You're a good cook!"

His father laughed. "Exams at school will be starting pretty soon now, won't they, son?"

"Monday."

His father lit his pipe and then picked up the paper again. He turned to the sports section. "Ready for 'em?" he asked.

"Guess so."

The room became silent. Alec turned more pages of his magazine, and then looked up at his father whose face was hidden behind the spread newspaper. Thick smoke curled upward toward the ceiling. Alec cleared his throat and was just about to speak when his father's voice broke the silence.

"All anybody can read in the sports section these days is news about that horse race out in Chicago next Saturday. Wonder who the devil this mystery horse is that Jim Neville's got into the race?"

Alec's pulses raced. "Dad——"

"Yes, son?"

"Dad, that's what I wanted to talk to you about. You see——"

His father once again let the paper fall on his lap and looked at him.

Alec couldn't keep his voice from faltering. "The mystery horse—the mystery horse," he stammered, "is the Black."

His father looked at his son in amazement. The room was still. "You mean, Alec, that the Black is the horse everyone's been talking about—he's the mystery horse?"

"That's right, Dad." Alec rose from his chair and went to the window; he drew the curtain to the side and then let it fall again.

"But who's going to ride him in a race like that?" Mr. Ramsay asked.

Alec tried to swallow, but nothing seemed to go down. "I am," he answered softly.

The doorbell rang. "I'll answer it, Dad," Alec said with relief. He knew it would be Henry answering his signal from the window.

Henry came in and removed his old brown hat. He gave Alec a knowing glance. "Evening, Mr. Ramsay," he said matter-of-factly.

"Hello, Henry," Alec's father answered. "Glad you're here. You must be in on this, too. Now tell me what the devil's been going on between you two and the Black? I had a hunch something was up but I never dreamed it was anything as stupendous as this!"

"It's quite a long story," Henry said. Then for the next half-hour he told about the training of the Black, and Alec's midnight rides at Belmont. Alec watched his father as he listened intently to Henry. How would he take it—he loved horses himself, but would he let him ride? It was a good thing Mom wasn't here!

When Henry finished, his father turned to him. "Leave us alone a few minutes, will you, Alec, please?"

Alec nodded and climbed the stairs to his room. Henry looked at Mr. Ramsay. "You've got to let him ride in that race," he said. "His heart and soul are wrapped up in it! Alec isn't the same boy that you sent to India last summer. You know that as well as I do. But he's a better man for it!"

"But, Henry, it's such a dangerous race for him to go into—and on that wild horse!"

"Not any more dangerous than what he's faced many times since that boat went down in the ocean. I've grown to know your boy pretty well within the last few months, and I can honestly say that he's different from any of us. He's found something that we never will, because we'll never go through the experiences that he's had to." Henry paused a few seconds. "Besides," he continued, "I'd be mighty proud to have a boy that could ride that black stallion—something, I'm certain, no one else in the world can do!"

Mr. Ramsay rose and walked across the room. He didn't say anything for a few minutes; then he walked toward the stairs. "Okay, Henry," he said. "I'll tell Alec he can ride!"

Jim Neville telephoned Henry the next day to tell him that everything was all set for the Black. The shipping charges to Chicago for the three horses would be taken care of from the proceeds of the race, as would all the rest of the charges to and from the track. Cyclone and Sun Raider were leaving Monday or Tuesday, so they could get in a couple of workouts before the race.

Henry couldn't tell him when the Black would be ready to leave; he had to ask Alec first.

"Whatever you do," Jim said, "don't run him over at Belmont any more. I'm trying to keep the mystery horse's identity a secret, because if it ever got out you'd be swarmed with reporters and it would only make the last few days all the more hectic. The Black is going to have enough excitement as it is!" Jim paused. "You're sure he's in good condition, Henry?" he asked. "Boy, I've gone way out on a limb with him. Got to wondering whether I'd been dreaming about that night—that's why I keep looking at this stopwatch in my desk drawer; it's the only thing that restores my confidence."

Henry laughed. "Sure," he said, "he's in tiptop shape!"

A few minutes after he had hung up, Alec came into the barn.

"Jim just called," Henry said. "Everything's all set for shipping the Black and stabling him out there—not going to be any expenses at all!" Henry looked out at the stallion in the field. "When can we shove off, Alec? Cyclone and Sun Raider are leaving tomorrow at the latest; that means they'll have a few days to get accustomed to the track."

"Just got through talking with Dad again," answered Alec. "He's letting me ride under one condition—that I stay until I finish my exams."

"How long is that?"

"I start 'em tomorrow and have my last one Thursday morning."

"Whew! And the race is Saturday," said Henry.

"Yes, and Dad insists we go out there by train. He called the station and found out there's a train that leaves Thursday afternoon that'll get us into Chicago early Friday morning. It's the only fair thing to do, Henry, and he has been swell about the whole thing."

"You're right, son. And that isn't so bad—gets us there a day ahead of time. Maybe it's just as well we aren't getting there too early, seeing it's the Black we're racin'."

Alec laid down his pen. There, his last exam was over! He blotted his paper carefully and looked up at the clock. Almost noon. He'd have to hurry if they were going to make the three o'clock train. He handed his paper to the teacher and walked out of the room.

In the hall he met Whiff and Bill. "How was it?" Bill asked.

"Not so bad," Alec replied, going right ahead. They fell into step with him.

"What's the hurry?" Whiff asked.

"Have to get home—some work to do," Alec answered. There was going to be plenty of work before they got the Black on the train.

"How're you comin' with the Black?" Whiff asked.

"Okay. Why don't you guys come around any more?"

"No, thanks," Whiff answered. "Not any more of that horse for me—he looks too dangerous!"

"Me, either," agreed Bill. "Talkin' about horses, how'd you like to be ridin' in that big race—day after tomorrow?"

Alec shrugged his shoulders.

"Should be a corker!" Bill went on. "Wonder who the mystery horse is going to turn out to be?"

"Probably some ham-and-egger," chirped up Whiff. "Cyclone will walk away with it."

"Not with Sun Raider in the race," Bill said. "Who do you think's going to win, Alec?"

Alec smiled. "Well, the only one you fellows leave me is the mystery horse—so I guess I'll take him."

"You're stuck," Bill laughed.

"We'll see," grinned Alec. He turned as he went out the door. "So long, fellas," he said.

"So long."

When he reached home, he found his father waiting for him. They didn't talk about the race while eating lunch. Then they went over to the barn. Alec wasn't nervous.

Instead he was calm and eager to match the Black's speed against Cyclone and Sun Raider.

In front of the barn Alec saw Henry and Jim Neville. Both of them were going to Chicago with Alec and the Black. Then there was Joe Russo and another man with a camera. Just to the side of them stood a large horse van. Alec and his father greeted the small group.

"Everything all set, Alec?" Henry asked.

"I suppose you took that exam in your stride today," Jim Neville kidded.

"Hope so," Alec answered. But his thoughts were turning forward. He nodded toward the van. "Guess we're going to the train in style, heh, Henry?"

"Sure!" Henry said. "And we're going out to Chicago in style, too. Jim tells me we have our own private car waiting for us at the station!"

"No!" Alec exclaimed.

"Yep. Isn't that so, Jim?"

"Yes," Jim replied. "Cyclone and Sun Raider got out to Chicago in special cars; there's no reason why the Black shouldn't. Besides, a lot of people are coming from far and wide to see these three horses, so they have to be at their best."

"That's fine with me," Alec said.

"Look what Jim gave us," Henry said. He held out a heavy, black horse blanket with a white border around it and white letters in the middle spelling THE BLACK.

"Gee, Jim, that's great," Alec said.

"Can't let 'em have anything on the Black." Jim smiled.

The stallion whinnied when Alec entered the barn. Alec took a soft cloth and wiped it over his large body. "Well, fella," he said, "we're off to the races." Henry tossed him the new blanket and Alec snapped it around the stallion. "There," he said proudly, "that'll keep you nice and warm."

"Sure makes him look like the real stuff," Henry said.

"He is the real stuff." Alec stroked the stallion's neck. Then he led him out of the barn. The Black reared when he saw the small crowd. Then he lifted his legs high and stepped gingerly in a circle.

"Let us take some pictures for the paper, will you, Alec?" Joe Russo asked.

"Sure," Alec answered. "Come on, Henry, you get into it, too."

Ten minutes passed while the photographer snapped pictures. Even Alec's father got into them. "Hope you'll be able to use these photos," Alec smiled, "after Saturday."

The Black reared again as the boy started to lead him up into the van. He neighed loudly and his head turned toward the barn; his ears pricked forward and his eyes shifted from Alec to the barn.

"What's the matter, fella?" Alec asked.

"I know," Henry said. "Every time we've put him into the truck, he's had Napoleon with him. Now he's wondering where he is!"

"You're right!" Alec said. "But we just have to get him in anyway. Come on, Black." But the stallion reared again, and when he came down he pushed his head into Alec's chest, shoving him back toward the barn.

"Napoleon isn't in there, fella," Alec said. "He's out working with Tony." But the Black only pushed harder.

Fifteen minutes later Alec was still trying to get him

into the van. "I'm afraid it's no use," he said. "When he gets his mind set on something, nobody's going to change it!"

Jim Neville glanced at his watch. "Getting late," he warned. "If we don't start within a few minutes, we'll never make the train—and there isn't another until tomorrow!"

"Black," Alec pleaded, "come on!" But the stallion only pranced around him, his nostrils quivering and his eyes looking for Napoleon. Suddenly his ears pricked forward. From far down the street came a familiar voice, "Apples, carrots, string beans, potatoes, cabbages, peas."

"It's Tony and Napoleon," Alec exclaimed. "They're on our street!"

"I'll get 'em," yelled Henry as he made a dash for the gate.

A few minutes later Napoleon loped down the street at his fastest trot. Tony and Henry sat in the seat of the wagon gripping the sides desperately as Napoleon dashed into the driveway.

The Black neighed loudly; his head turned toward them. Napoleon's old legs made the gravel fly. He rushed to the Black and shoved his nose up at him.

Tony and Henry jumped off the seat. *"Dio mio,"* exclaimed Tony, "what's-a da matta with heem?"

Henry told Tony how they had taken Napoleon with them when they trained the Black at Belmont and how now the Black was going to run in the big match race in Chicago. "And now, Tony," Henry finished, "we can't get him in the van because we're not taking Napoleon."

Jim Neville spoke up. "Tony," he said, "would it be all

right with you if we took Napoleon with us to the race?"

Alec began to feel more hopeful. "Do you think we could, Jim?" he asked.

"Sure, if Tony'll let us. There's plenty of room on the train, and we're sure to find a stable for him out there. What do you say, Tony? We'll have him back to you by Sunday night, or Monday at the latest. And to make everything square, we'll pay you for Napoleon's time!"

Tony looked at Napoleon standing with his head beside the Black's. He was silent a minute; then his dark face creased into a grin. "Sure," he said, "why not? But no money, thanks please. He's been-a da good horse for fifteen years—now he's gonna have da vacation."

"Atta boy, Tony," Alec said. "It's going to mean a lot to the Black—and to us, too."

"You betcha," Tony said proudly, as he put a caressing hand on Napoleon's neck.

"And now," said Jim Neville, "let's get going."

Henry led Napoleon up into the van and Alec followed with the Black. He was as docile now as he had been difficult before.

A few minutes later they rolled down the driveway. Alec sat between Henry and Jim. They waved to the small group standing beside the barn.

"Good luck," yelled Joe Russo.

"Be careful, son," his father called. "And put everything you've got into it!"

"Take-a da good care of my Napoleon," Tony shouted.

Then they went through the gate.

"We're off," said Henry.

Chicago

17

It was two-thirty by Jim's watch when they drove into the freight yards. "Just in time," he said.

Trucks laden with freight for the trains pulled into the yards, their horns blowing. Men's shouts rang through the afternoon air. Henry brought the van to a stop. "I'll find out where we're to go," Jim said. "Wait here."

Alec looked back through the window. He could see the heads of the Black and Napoleon. The stallion was pawing at the floor. "Guess the noise and the ride's made him kinda nervous, Henry," he said.

"Yeah, we'll have to watch him. Wouldn't want him to get too excited just before the race."

A few minutes later Jim returned. "Our car's down at the end," he said. Henry put the truck in gear and moved in and out of the crowded yards. Jim pointed to a car. "That's the one."

"I can back right up to the door," Henry said, as he turned the wheel. "He'll hardly know he's getting into it."

When Henry brought the van to a stop, Jim and Alec jumped out. They climbed into the train and Henry followed them. "Say, this is swell!" Alec said as he looked around him. A box stall was at one end and three cots were in front of it.

"Not a bad layout," agreed Henry. "The Black won't mind this so much."

"We haven't a stall for Napoleon, though," Jim said.

"We can put him right outside the Black's," Henry said, "and move our cots down this way."

After they'd moved the cots and Henry had bedded down the stallion's stall with straw, Alec went to get the Black.

He opened the rear of the van and walked in beside him. The Black moved nervously. "Hello, fella." Alec stroked his neck. Napoleon pushed his face toward him and Alec rubbed his nose too. "You're both going on a long ride now," he said. He grasped the Black's halter and backed him into the stall. The horse stretched his neck high into the air and his leg continued to paw the straw. "There, Boy," Alec said. "Take it easy, now."

"Don't bring Napoleon in yet," Henry said. "I'll need more straw if we're going to bed him down and make him comfortable. I'll go see if I can't get some."

"I'll go along with you, Henry," Jim said. "I have to make arrangements to get this van back."

As soon as they had gone, Alec went inside the van and dragged Henry's large trunk into the car. He opened it and took out Henry's blazing green shirt and jockey cap. Saturday he'd be wearing them! The same things even to the faded Number 3 that Henry had worn when he and Chang won the Kentucky Derby! Alec's throat tightened as he laid them carefully back into the trunk.

A short time later, Henry returned with a bale of straw. He spread it in front of the Black's stall. "Okay to bring Napoleon in now," he said. Napoleon's ears pricked forward when he saw the Black. He shoved his nose toward him.

Jim climbed into the car. "Everything's set," he said.

Fifteen minutes later the train whistle blew.

"Chicago, here we come," Alec shouted.

He tossed on his cot that night. The clattering of the wheels on the iron rails kept him awake. He heard the Black moving restlessly around in his stall. Alec rose and made his way quietly over to him. Henry's and Jim's deep breathing told him that they were both sound asleep. Napoleon, too, was sleeping.

The Black whinnied when he saw the boy. "Shh, fella." Alec rubbed the stallion's head.

The train rocked a little, and the Black shied. "Not any worse than a boat, though, is it?" Alec asked. The Black shook his head. For fifteen minutes Alec stayed with him. Then he gave a final pat. "Gotta try and get some sleep now, fella—we both need it."

He went back to his cot and lay down. He dozed off. He was dreaming of the coming race. Then he opened his eyes and stared at the ceiling. He had to quit thinking. He must get some sleep. He tried to concentrate on the rhythmic beat of the wheels on the rails. They seemed to say, "Chicago—Chicago—Chicago——" Alec dropped off to sleep.

The next thing he knew, Henry was shaking him. Both

he and Jim were already dressed. "We're almost there," Henry said.

Alec pulled on his clothes sleepily.

"How do you feel, kid?" Jim asked.

"All right," answered Alec.

"We're entering the city limits now," Henry said.

"How far is the track from the station?" Alec asked.

Jim looked at his watch. "About a forty-five-minute ride," he said. "It's five-thirty now; if the van I hired is waiting for us, we'll be at the track by six-thirty at the latest."

"Let's hope it's there," Henry said. "It'll be better if we can get to the track before any people start roaming around."

The train pulled into the freight yards. Alec snapped the Black's new blanket around him. Henry took care of Napoleon. As the train slowed down, Jim pushed the door of the car open. Trucks clattered beside the train. "Bad as New York," Henry said.

"I'll see if I can find our van," Jim said, jumping off the train as it came to a stop.

The Black moved uneasily and Alec held him tighter. Henry moved Napoleon over closer to him. The stallion's startled eyes gazed nervously out the open door, then quieted as Napoleon shoved his head toward him.

A van moved alongside the car. Then they heard Jim's voice. "Back it up to the door," he directed the driver.

A few minutes later Alec led the Black into the van, followed by Henry and Napoleon.

The early morning streets were deserted, and they made good time to the track. They passed the huge stands and then pulled into the gate entrance near the stables.

The gatekeeper hailed them. "What do you want?" he asked.

Jim spoke up. "I'm Jim Neville," he said. "We've a horse here—for the race tomorrow."

"The mystery horse, heh?" The gatekeeper smiled. "We've been waiting for him!" He swung the gate open. "Take any stall you want in Barn H," he yelled at them. "Just don't get too close to Sun Raider and Cyclone Still," he chuckled, "perhaps you'd better get close to 'em now—'cause you won't tomorrow! Haw."

"Humorous sort of a guy, isn't he?" Jim said.

"He'll change his tune," said Henry.

Alec peered back through the window at the Black. The stallion's head was still shoved toward Napoleon's.

Fifteen minutes later, they had the Black in his new quarters. They put Napoleon in the empty stall next to him. The track seemed deserted in the early morning stillness.

"Guess no visitors are allowed," Alec said.

"Cyclone and Sun Raider must be up the barn a ways," Henry answered. "The men in their stables will be around, soon as they hear we've arrived."

"And you won't be able to keep the newspaper men out of here today," reminded Jim.

"We've got to keep them away from the Black, or there's no telling what will happen," Henry said.

Alec and Henry then busied themselves around the barn making the stallion and Napoleon comfortable while Jim went to see Cyclone and Sun Raider. Sponges, cloths, brushes were unpacked.

Henry looked up and saw a crowd of men making their way toward them. "Here they come," he said to Alec.

Henry walked out of the stall to meet them, leaving Alec with the Black. He saw the group was composed of reporters and stable hands as Jim had warned. "Morning," Henry greeted them.

"We've come to see the wonder horse," one man said, laughing.

"You mean the mystery horse," another corrected him.

"There he is," Henry said, pointing to the Black, whose excited eyes gazed at them.

Alec stroked his head. "Take it easy, fella," he said.

Some of the men started coming closer.

"You'll have to keep away from his stall," Henry said, stopping them. "He's excitable and we want to keep him quiet."

"Temperamental, heh?" a reporter sneered.

Henry's Irish temper started rising. "No more cracks," he said. "If you don't like it where you're standing, I'll throw you out of here!"

The men saw that Henry meant it, and they kept away from the short, stocky figure.

After a few minutes, they broke up. "Maybe he won't be so cocky after tomorrow," said a stable hand.

"Don't know how he got in this race, anyway!" said another.

A short while later Jim came back. "Sun Raider and Cyclone look like they're in good condition," he said. "Why don't you two go over and see them? I'll keep an eye on the Black."

"Guess we will," said Henry. "Come on, Alec."

First they went to Cyclone's stables. There was a crowd in front, and Henry and Alec mingled with it without being recognized. Cyclone was led out of his stall so the photographers could take pictures of him.

He was a big horse—almost as big as the Black! His coat shone a bright red in the morning sun. He moved gracefully around in a circle. His head was larger than the Black's, and his eyes didn't have that tense, savage look.

"You can tell he's Kentucky born and bred," Henry whispered. "He's built for speed all the way."

Alec nodded. "He sure is streamlined," he said.

They watched while the photographers took shots of him. Then they went up the line toward Sun Raider's stable. They saw him as he was coming in off the track. Alec gasped—he was just about as big and powerful-looking as the Black! His coat was chestnut gold. His head was small and his neck rose in a crest like the Black's.

"Gee," Alec said, "he almost looks like the Black."

"Yeah," whispered Henry. "He might prove to be the one we'll have to beat. But we can't forget Cyclone," he said as he jerked his head backwards. "That horse has never been pushed to his top speed; he runs only fast enough to win."

"They're both going to be tough to beat," Alec said.

"The fastest in the world—take my word for it," Henry said. "But we knew what we were getting into."

"I still think the Black can beat them," Alec said.

The Match Race

18

The day of the big race! The eyes of the nation turned upon Chicago. All morning long trains, buses, autos and planes roared into the city discharging thousands of passengers bound for the track.

A carnival spirit swept over the city. Everything was closed for the day, and everywhere one question was asked, "Who will win—Cyclone or Sun Raider?"

"How're you doin', Charlie?" asked a motorcycle cop of a policeman who was directing traffic at one of Chicago's busiest corners, as he pulled up beside him.

"Never saw anything like it, Pat!" came the answer. "Where the devil they all coming from?" Horns blew from the endless lines of cars that stretched far down the avenues.

"I'm worn out myself. They're just about packed solid from here to the track. They'll never get all of 'em inside!"

"They're comin' from all over the country to see this race. Boy, I'd like to be up there myself—to see Cyclone lick 'em!"

The motorcycle cop kicked his motor over. "So would I," he yelled above the roar. "But it's going to be Sun Raider by three lengths!"

"We'll see. Say, what do you think of this mystery horse?"

"Nothin' much—guess everyone's beginning to wonder how he got in the race anyway. He won't figure in it at all—that's inside stuff! See you later. . . ."

In a large apartment house, not far from the track, Alec's mother and his Aunt Bess looked out the large living-room window at the slow-moving traffic below them. In the distance they could see the track already jammed with people.

"Bess, did you ever see such traffic in all your life?" Mrs. Ramsay asked. "What on earth is happening over there?"

"Don't tell me that you haven't heard about the big match race that's being run today. Everyone has been talking about it. Why, I even bought box seat tickets. I was going to surprise you!"

"But, Bess, I've never seen a horse race in my life. I won't know what it's all about!"

"There's nothing to it." Her sister laughed. "The horse that gets around the track first wins! I don't go myself much, but this is something nobody should miss. For the first and only time Sun Raider and Cyclone are going to meet. You've heard of them. It'll probably be the grandest horse race of all times. And if you think we're not going to see it when we only live a quarter of a mile away from the track, why—" She looked out of the window. "Look at those crowds! Come, Belle, let's get our hats and coats and go so that we get our seats."

Mrs. Ramsay shook her head as she went for her hat and coat. "If my husband or son ever finds out about my seeing this race, I won't have a moment's peace when I get home. I'll have to take that horse of Alec's right into the house! I told you, Bess, how they're both so crazy over him. I have all I can do now to keep everything under control. . . . They'd certainly love to see this race!

"It's too bad they're not here, but they are always too busy to have any fun. . . ."

A plane dropped out of the cloudless sky. Swiftly it circled the field and then came roaring down and rolled to a stop.

The passengers hurried toward the door. "Just about time to make it, if we hurry," one of them said.

The stewardess called, "Bus is waiting directly ahead to take you to the track!" The passengers sprinted for the car.

Alec's father darted into a seat behind the driver. "Think we'll get there before they start?" he asked.

"Yeah, I think so. They always take some time getting those temperamental babies on the track!" the driver answered.

"Sun Raider always puts up a terrific fight beforehand anyway," the man who slipped into the seat next to him said. "He's a lot wilder than Cyclone."

"Might as well do his fighting then," said a man behind them. "He won't be anywhere near Cyclone once they're off!"

"Oh, yeah? It'll be Sun Raider by two lengths today!" He turned to Mr. Ramsay. "Who do you think is going to win?" he asked.

"I'm picking the mystery horse."

"Say, don't you know that's a publicity stunt," the man answered. "I'll bet you there won't even be a third horse out there today!"

"We'll see," Alec's father said. "We'll see."

Alec stroked the Black. "It's almost time, fella," he said. The stallion pawed at the straw. Outside a line of policemen kept the eager spectators away. In the distance Alec could see the stands jammed with people. Band music drifted toward them. Henry came back from looking over the track.

"Fast as the devil," he said. "Better go over and check it out for yourself," he said. He stopped and his eyes blinked a little as he put a hand on the green shirt Alec wore. "Fits pretty good, doesn't it?" He smiled.

"Swell," Alec answered. "So do the pants and the cap." He put on the cap and pulled the long peak down over his eyes to show Henry.

Henry straightened the Number 3 on Alec's arm. "They'll bring you luck," he said. "They did me. . . ."

Alec was on his way back from the track when he passed the two jockeys who were riding Cyclone and Sun Raider. They looked much older than they did in the pictures he had seen in the newspapers.

One of them saw him. "Say, you're the kid with the mystery horse, aren't you?"

Alec nodded.

"So you're actually going to ride in this race!" Sun

Raider's jockey grinned. "We thought you were just part of a publicity gag, didn't we, Dave?"

The other jockey pulled him by the arm. "Come on," he said, "quit wastin' time." Then he looked at Alec. "Better take it easy in this race, kid." They turned and walked away.

Alec's anger mounted as he walked toward the stables. Who did those guys think they were, anyway! Just because they were old hands at this game they thought they owned the track.

Henry had the Black out of his stall when he got back. "All set, kid?" he asked.

"All set."

The noise from the distance made the stallion nervous. Alec rubbed his neck.

"Just a few things I want you to remember, Alec," Henry continued. "There isn't much to tell you about handling the Black—you know more about him than I do. You're a good rider, and I've taught you all the tricks I know—now, it's up to you to put them in use. Those other two jockeys are the slickest riders in the game. They won't let you get away with a thing—but they won't try anything that's outside the rules; they're smart but not dirty. They're out to win, but so are you. Remember you've got all the horse under you that they have."

"I'm sure of that, Henry," Alec interrupted as he looked proudly at the Black.

"I can't tell you to hold him back," Henry continued, "because you won't be able to. Stay on him and ride like you never have before! If the Black's the kind of a horse we've been figuring him to be, he should win all the way!"

Cyclone was the first out of the barn for the big race. He received lusty cheers on his way to the paddock. He was draped in a flaming red robe and wore red blinkers.

A few minutes later Sun Raider was led from the barn almost wholly concealed in a white woolen blanket. He pranced nervously and his small head turned viciously around. Another cheer went up from the crowd gathered around the paddock rail when they saw him.

Then a hush fell upon the crowd as the Black appeared, covered in his new black robe and accompanied by old Napoleon. Alec held him by the lead rope attached to his halter. The stallion reared and Alec let the rope slip through his fingers until he came down. The Black's eyes blazed when he saw the other stallions. Alec remembered the fight the Black had had with the chestnut stallion in Rio. He tightened his grip on the rope and walked him far behind the others when they reached the paddock stalls.

The silence was broken by a man's loud yell, "There's the mystery horse!" Then everyone started talking. They hadn't expected to see anything like the Black. "He's even bigger than Sun Raider!" Alec heard one man exclaim.

A few minutes later one of the track officials called, "Riders up!"

The blankets were whipped off the horses. Henry saddled and bridled the Black and then boosted Alec into the saddle. "Let the others get out first, so there won't be any trouble," he said, as they went slowly around the paddock ring. The Black's gaze was on the horses far ahead of him. His nostrils quivered and he shook his head nervously. Alec knew that only Napoleon beside him kept him under control.

A long line of policemen kept the crowd back and made a path from the paddock to the track. The bugle sounded. The Black raised his head and his ears pricked forward. Henry led him toward the track.

They stopped at the entrance to the track. Cyclone and Sun Raider were already walking past the grandstand on their way to the post. Henry looked up at Alec. "Well, kid, you're on your own now," he said quietly. "Go to it!"

Alec's heart pounded as he saw the solid mass of people stretched out before him. "Okay, Henry," he said. Old Napoleon neighed plaintively as Henry kept him from following the Black out on the track.

Every vantage point in and around the outer fences of the course was jammed with excited fans. Many perched on roof tops fully a mile from the starting point. Their attention was focused on Sun Raider and Cyclone as they passed the stands. Then suddenly they saw a giant black horse, his mane waving like windblown flame, coming down the track. Spectators rose in their seats and excited hands raised glasses to their eyes.

"It's the mystery horse!" shouted a well-known sports commentator to a network audience. "He's listed as the Black and ridden by Alec Ramsay. He's raising quite a commotion around here! He's one of the biggest horses that I've ever seen—if not *the* biggest. He's black, coal black. He's big and strong and doesn't seem to want to go near the other horses. Alec Ramsay on his back is having a very difficult time controlling him. Lord! I've seen plenty of horses in my time, but none with action like that! I'd say that this horse that most of us have labeled 'Neville's Folly' is going to be very much in the picture of this race. Yes, sir, it's shaping up to be the greatest match race of all time or I miss my guess!

"Now he's approaching the post. Cyclone doesn't want to go near him and moves away. Sun Raider stands his ground and his teeth are bared. The starter's having quite a time. That black horse is a devil! He wants to fight! They're lining up. There he goes up into the air! He's plunging at Sun Raider, striking! Listen to that black devil scream—never in my life have I heard anything like it! It's risen to such a high pitch that it's practically a whistle—you probably all can hear it! There, Alec Ramsay's got him down—that boy sure can stick on a horse. What a struggle is going on out there, folks! Over eighty thousand people here, and I can say without fear of contradiction, they've never seen anything like this before! Take it from me the Black is a wild stallion— never clearly broken. A savage on the race track!

"You folks who have seen Sun Raider know that they don't often come much wilder, but he's certainly met his match today—in fighting, anyway! He's backing away from the Black now! They've got Cyclone in between the two of them. That's better. Alec Ramsay is managing the Black now. That boy is doing wonders—I wouldn't be in his shoes for all the money in the world! Sun Raider won't stand still. He's furious—he hates the Black. He's broken out of line. There he goes striking at the Black! He's hit him! Oh, oh, the Black's leg is bleeding—that was a pretty hard blow. Alec Ramsay can't hold his horse any longer—he's on his hind legs and plunging at Sun Raider. There's no way of stopping this thing! Sun Raider is backing up again—he doesn't stand a chance with that black devil! Wait, there's Alec Ramsay pulling on his horse's head—he's turning him off. He's getting him under control again. He's got him on the outside. Sun Raider doesn't want to fight any more. He's back at his position on the pole.

"Looks as though the starter is going to send them off—while he's got them there. The Black's leg is bleeding pretty badly. Sun Raider doesn't seem to be much the worse off for the fight. Alec Ramsay is leaning over looking at the Black's wound. He's getting off—he'll probably leave the race, too bad——*They're off!* The starter wasn't watching Alec Ramsay—he was climbing out of his saddle.

"Cyclone and Sun Raider are fighting head and head as they flash past the stands. The Black is left at the post; he's out of the race. No, no, here he comes after them! His jockey is only half in the saddle. Now he's on! He's trying desperately to pull the Black to a stop; he doesn't want him to run with his leg in that condition. He's pulling furiously on the reins, but it doesn't seem to be doing any good. The Black wants to run—he's fighting for his head! He's almost pulling Alec Ramsay straight up in his saddle. Now he's ripped the reins out of his hands! He's close to a hundred yards behind, too far to catch up—but he's going to run!

"Cyclone has beaten Sun Raider to the first turn— they're both running under the whip. Each wants to set the pace! Cyclone's jockey is deliberately pulling his horse up, so that Cyclone's churning hindquarters are right in Sun Raider's nose. That's a shrewd move as it gives his mount a breather after that stretch sprint and forces Sun Raider to check his speed from running on Cyclone's heels!

"But now as they round the turn, Sun Raider, the

California comet, is moving up alongside Cyclone, and as they enter the backstretch they're running neck and neck——"

Suddenly a deafening roar rose from the stands. "Look, look," yelled the commentator hysterically. "The Black is coming up like a house on fire! You've never in your life seen a horse run like this! He's all power—all beauty. The distance between him and the others is lessening. How it's lessening! I wouldn't believe it if I wasn't seeing it with my own eyes. The Black is running the others down! Cyclone and Sun Raider are fighting for the lead going into the last turn. The Black's almost behind them. What action! What a tremendous stride! The crowd is going crazy. Sun Raider is passing Cyclone on the turn and going into the lead! Here they come down the homestretch——"

The crowd began to scream as the fighting horses came thundering toward them. Sun Raider was surging ahead. Cyclone was falling back—the Black had him! Sun Raider was two lengths in front, his jockey batting away with his whip. The Black started moving up. Now he was a length behind. No whip was being used on him—his jockey was like a small burr lost in the stallion's thick, black mane.

Hysteria swept the crowd as the horses passed them for the second time—the finish wire only one hundred yards away. "He'll never get Sun Raider!" yelled the sportscaster. The stallion flashed by the stands, going faster with every magnificent stride. With a sudden spurt he bore down on Sun Raider. For a moment he hesitated as he came alongside. The crowd gasped as the Black's ears went back and he bared his teeth. There was a movement on his back; his jockey's hand rose and fell on the stallion's side for the first time in the race. Into the lead the Black swept, past the cheering thousands—a step, a length, two lengths ahead—then the mighty giant plunged under the wire.

The Black rounded the first turn and had entered the backstretch again before Alec was able to slow him down. He knew that only the pain in the stallion's leg enabled him to do it then. Finally he brought him to a stop.

Alec forgot the cheering thousands as he slid, exhausted, from the stallion's back. He bent down to look at the wound. There was so much blood! Alec took his handkerchief and wrapped it around the Black's leg to try to stop the bleeding. "You shouldn't have done it, Boy," he said.

A station wagon roared around the track toward them, leaving a cloud of dust in its wake. The Black reared as it pulled up to them. Henry and another man jumped out.

"Is he hurt much?" he asked Alec anxiously. "Here's the track veterinary——"

"Can't tell. It's bleeding pretty bad and I know it's hurting him!"

The veterinary bent down to examine the wound. Henry went to the wagon and returned carrying a pail of water, sponge and bandage. The veterinary cut off Alec's handkerchief, which was now covered with blood.

The voices of the clamoring thousands stilled, as they realized what was happening on the track. All eyes were upon the small group.

The veterinary straightened up. "He's lost a lot of blood, but it's only a superficial wound. Nothing to worry about. Give him a rest and he'll be as good as new!"

Alec and Henry looked at each other and their eyes were moist. No word was spoken while the veterinary bandaged the Black's leg. Then Henry broke the silence. "Well, Alec," he said, "guess you and the Black did it!"

The veterinary stood up. "Okay," he said. "And now I think they're waiting for you over at the winner's circle."

As Henry boosted the boy into the saddle, an avalanche of cheers rose from the crowd. The stallion's ears pricked forward and he looked wildly around. Alec patted him on the neck. For the first time he realized that the race was over, that they had won. "You did it, Boy," he said proudly. "You did it!" The blood raced through his veins and his heart pounded against his ribs as the crowd cheered them on their way back. The stallion reared as they approached the grandstand.

Thousands of pairs of eyes watched the Black as he pranced out there beyond the crowd. He did not want to come closer. Yet he did not seem to fight his rider. Some of the crowd broke through the police line and rushed toward him. They stopped suddenly when he reared, and moved back quickly as he came toward them, head and tail erect. His action was beautiful, springy, and every few steps he jumped with marvelous ease and swiftness. Experts shook their heads knowingly at the Black's performance. "Here," said one old man, "is the greatest horse that ever set foot on any track!"

Alec rode the Black up to the judges' stand, and into the winner's circle. The stallion stood still for the first time. Alec and Henry could hardly believe their eyes. Even flashlight bulbs exploding close at hand only caused him to toss his head. They put the horseshoe of roses around his neck.

Alec looked around at the crowd below him. Suddenly he stopped—could that be his father? "Dad," he yelled. "Dad!" His father turned and waved. "Henry—look! There's Dad over there!"

Henry pushed his way through the crowd and was halfway back with Alec's father when a familiar voice made them both turn.

"Looks as though we're all here!" said Alec's mother.

"Belle!" gasped Mr. Ramsay.

She put a hand on her husband's arm. "I've never had such an afternoon in all my life," she said. "From the time I saw Alec come out on the Black and couldn't do anything about it, until the end." She paused and looked at Alec sitting proudly astride his horse. "But now all I care about is that it's over and he's safe."

"We all should be mighty proud of him," Henry said as he led the way toward Alec.

The governor of the state had just given Alec the Gold Trophy emblematic of track supremacy when Alec saw both his father and his mother with Henry. His mouth dropped open, and he forgot to listen to the governor, who was talking to him. He wasn't seeing things—they were *both* there! He waved; his throat was too tight to say anything. The governor kept talking. The Black shook his head and pawed the ground.

Finally the governor was through. The crowd cheered and Alec slid off the Black. Henry unsaddled the stallion. Suddenly a line of policemen pushed through the crowd. Following them came Jim Neville leading Napoleon. The stallion whinnied and threw his head high into the air. Old Napoleon answered and thrust his nose up to the Black's. "Nice going, kid!" said Jim. "I knew you two could do it!" He nodded at Napoleon. "He was almost going crazy back there—wanted to do a little congratulating himself!"

"He belongs up here, anyway." Alec laughed.

The network sportscaster pushed his way through and

rushed up to Alec. "—broke the world's record!" he was telling his audience. Then he pushed the mike in front of Alec and motioned for him to say something.

Alec hesitated a moment. "The Black was every bit as good as we believed him to be," he said. "We knew he had it in him, and he proved it today!"

The sportscaster then broke in and started giving the history of Alec and the Black. Jim Neville had told him the whole story.

The owners of Sun Raider and Cyclone came up and congratulated Alec. "I've never seen anything like him as long as I've been around the track," Mr. Volence said.

"That goes for me, too!" said Mr. Hurst. "I don't suppose you'd consider selling him?"

"No, sir." Alec answered proudly. "You're going to hear a lot more about this fella!"

"I'm afraid of that," laughed Cyclone's owner.

Answering the pleas of the hundreds grouped around them, Alec took a few roses from the huge bow of flowers draped around the Black's neck, and then threw the rest of them into the throng. In a few seconds the souvenir hunters had ripped them apart.

The Black half-reared and old Napoleon moved closer to him. Alec smiled at Henry and his mother and father. He rubbed the Black's nose, and then led the huge stallion through the crowd—back to his victory oats.

ABOUT THE AUTHOR

WALTER FARLEY's love for horses began when he was a small boy living in Syracuse, New York, and continued as he grew up in New York City, where his family moved. Unlike most city children, he was able to fulfill this love through an uncle who was a professional horseman. Young Walter spent much of his time with this uncle, learning about the different kinds of horse training and the people associated with each.

Walter Farley began to write his first book, *The Black Stallion*, while he was a student at Brooklyn's Erasmus Hall High School and Mercersburg Academy in Pennsylvania. He finished it and had it published in 1941 while he was still an undergraduate at Columbia University.

The appearance of *The Black Stallion* brought such an enthusiastic response from young readers that Mr. Farley went on to create more stories about the Black, and about other horses as well. In his life he wrote a total of thirty-four books, including *Man o' War*, the story of America's greatest Thoroughbred, and two photographic storybooks based on the two Black Stallion movies. His books have been enormously popular in the United States and have been published in twenty-one foreign countries.

Mr. Farley and his wife, Rosemary, had four children, whom they raised on a farm in Pennsylvania and in a beach house in Florida. Horses, dogs, and cats were always a part of the household.

In 1989 Mr. Farley was honored by his hometown library in Venice, Florida, which established the Walter Farley Literary Landmark in its children's wing. Mr. Farley died in October 1989, shortly before publication of *The Young Black Stallion*, the twenty-first book in the Black Stallion series.